I Exist.

THEREFORE I AM

By the Same Author

Short Stories

Breaking News (Vijitha Yapa, 2011. Self Published, 2017, 2018)

Poetry

Chant of a Million Women (Self Published, 2017)

Praise for *Breaking News*

A 2010 Gratiaen Award Shortlist

"Each story in the collection is located within a different social milieu, and yet, the author manages to do justice to each different social background she portrays. When she describes situations in which the main characters are the victims of violence, she manages to convey to the reader their emotions in powerfully descriptive language, which is poetic and nuanced. She does not merely use a linear narrative style but experiments with literary devices like flashbacks and at times employs overarching metaphors in some of her stories."

- *Judges' Comments, Gratiaen Award 2010, Sri Lanka*

"Humorous or heartbreaking, plain prose or philosophical, Rajapakse shows immense talent in this collection of stories. Readers will find it easy to finish the book in a single setting, but they will find it difficult to forget Rajapakse's elegant turn of phrase and the depth with which she tackles her plots and characters. While the majority of the media may focus on more prominent wars and military conflicts, the defeat of the Tamil Tigers marked the beginning of a new era in Sri Lanka and Rajapakse does her native country complete justice (and then some) with *Breaking News*."

- *Ekta R. Garg, Bookpleasures, USA*

"The language is simple and unadorned, marked by a starkness exactly appropriate to the subject matter. The stories contain oblique descriptions of people and places, but pain and loss form the major chord in these related arias."

- *Luke Sherwood, Basso Profundo, USA*

Praise for *Chant of a Million Women*

A 2018 Kindle Book Awards Winner

A 2018 Readers' Favorite Awards Honorable Mention

A 2018 New Apple Summer eBook Awards for Excellence in Independent Publishing Official Selection

"Overall this collection is spirited and powerful, and above all, it has an important message that is expressed so well. This is one of my favourite collections I've reviewed so far, and I would thoroughly recommend it."

- *Sam Rose, Peeking Cat Poetry Magazine, UK*

"Men in power twisting rules regarding women's reproductive rights is something that all women, regardless of socioeconomic status, race, creed, can relate to. Touching on topics like these makes Rajapakse's poetry universal. While her language takes the reader on a journey filled with beauty inside of the darkness of the topics."

- *Jessica Wright, Poetry International, USA*

"This is a distinctive, consistent collection in which the milk of human kindness has no place. Nowhere are the kind whispers of a lover or even the support of a life partner. Ms Rajapakse has consistently chosen her pieces with a eye to the plaints and sorrows of women. I salute the courage with which she lends her voice for the forgotten and uncared-for women suffering in so many places in the world. Take up Chant of a Million Women and experience its elegant phrases and its moral force."

- *Luke Sherwood, Basso Profundo, USA*

"This is a collection that voices the female experience and how men and women relate to each other, all the while set to Rajapakse's musical cadence and word choices."

- *Suzanna Anderson, Magnolia Review, USA*

"There were times when I felt embarrassed for the way that our society has taught people to behave. Not all of these poems were particularly enjoyable in their experience, but every one of them sparked thought and brought up very real questions that we should all be considering. That is the true value in this work. It is not a light read. It is not something you'd carry with you to the beach or enjoy over a night, relaxing vacation. There's nothing relaxing about this. This is a book that sparks movement, that demands action. If you are prepared to be dragged into a reality that most of us would prefer to ignore, this is a great way to do it. Let these words show you the things you haven't learned yet. Let them make you angry. Let them draw you out and call you to action. Well done, Shirani. This is a powerful collection, and I hope it calls forth the action and attention it deserves."

- *Bobbie Stanley, A Page to Turn, USA*

"Beautiful and moving poetry"

- *Madeleine Black, Author of "Unbroken"*

"Chant of a Million Women is correctly classified as poetry about women's issues. No argument there. But in my opinion, it is just as accurately, and perhaps even more pointedly, poetry about men."

"Rajapakse's poems are clearly aimed at those who don't, and who often justify their exploitation, disrespect and brutality by the attractiveness of their victims. She defiantly reminds them of their hypocrisy. And she sadly reminds us all of the terrible waste of so many lives to hopelessness and despair. "That's why I write, I whisper to the winds." Highly recommended."

- *Kimberlee J Benart, Readers' Favorite, USA*

"My personal guidelines, when doing an 'official' KBR review, are as follows: five stars means, roughly equal to best in genre. Rarely given. Four stars means, extremely good. Three stars means, definitely recommendable. I am a tough reviewer. I try to be consistent. Rajapakse has great range in this book, writing with power and control. You will find your own favourites here, as well as those mentioned above. Five stars feels right on. Highly recommended."

- *Jim Bennett, Kindle Book Review Team member, Canada*

"I was pleasantly surprised by the raw beauty of this selection of poems by the acclaimed poet Shirani Rajapakse. This collection adds to her growing reputation. Through her poems the lonely, the downtrodden and the abused have found a voice, and a champion. Read it. Be moved by it."

- *Manoj Krishna, Author of "Understanding Me Understanding You: An Enquiry into Being Human"*

"The power, pride and confidence displayed within Shirani's poetry is captivating and overwhelming. I felt connected to many of her words and could feel the poems as though they were written with my life in mind. Women of all generations and ethnic backgrounds would be able to relate, in some way, to the poems and words expressed!"

- *Vanessa M. Thibeault, Author of "All of Me, All of You'*

"Very hard to beat is the poetic sincerity and strongly felt emotion running through this collection. The collection succeeds because it provokes profound reflection on what it means, and what it has meant to be a woman in a mainly patriarchal, repressive world."

- *Lynn Ockersz, The Island, Sri Lanka*

"Shirani Rajapakse provides a captivating insight into all corners of the female psyche. All women, from queens to the ordinary woman are vividly present in her pages.

Indeed, Rajapakse provides a very coherent and full collection with many recurrent themes thoughtfully contrasting and complementing each other.

However, most importantly, not one voice appears more highly or lowly than another. They stand as equals, speaking to the reader in unison and creating a powerful chant as one."

- *Daljinder Johal, DESIblitz, UK*

"Rajapakse's work is filled with astute observation and insight."

- *Jose Angel Araguz, The Friday Influence, USA*

I Exist.

THEREFORE I AM

SHIRANI RAJAPAKSE

Published by Shirani Rajapakse

Copyright © 2018 Shirani Rajapakse

The right of Shirani Rajapakse to be identified as the author of this work has been asserted by her in accordance with International Copyright Treaties and Conventions.

This is a work of fiction. The names, characters, place and incidents portrayed in them – save where obviously genuine - are the work of the author's imagination. Any resemblance to actual persons, living or dead, events or localities, is entirely coincidental.

Cover concept by Shirani Rajapakse
Cover image and design by FayeFayeDesigns
fiverr.com/fayefayedesigns

First Published in 2018

Paperback: ISBN 978-955-38285-3-8
eBook: ISBN 978-955-38285-4-5

1. Short Stories. 2. Fiction—21st century. 3. Women. 4. Literary Fiction. 5. Woman—abuse. 6. Asian Writer. 7. Shirani Rajapakse.

For information about permission to reproduce selections from this book, or to translate, write to

shiraniraj@hotmail.com

shiranirajapakse@gmail.com

shiranirajapakse.wordpress.com

Contents

Introduction

Introduction

I've travelled in India more times than I have any other country. Although the first few visits were for adventure and I did the usual touristic trails, I also went off the beaten track to explore places others wouldn't venture on a tour. Years later I moved there for study and soon after for work. I used that time for more exploration, mostly for fun but also to discover the places that intrigued me.

I like meeting people and learning about their life, their hopes and how they cope. People aren't very different around the world; we all want to be happy, lead good lives and enjoy the little pleasures along the way. What makes us different is the way we look at life and what it throws at us. This is sometimes hard to do as attitudes and social practices tend to change our perceptions depending on the places we come from.

The stories in this collection are just that – stories They were written at two stages of my life and represents the eight years I spent in India, working and travelling to cities and also some of the remote places where I encountered many instances of negativity towards women and girls. Some of the incidents I came across or heard about are too painful to recount or fictionalize. The tales I have included here are a mere fraction of the lives touched during my stay.

While the incidents portrayed like rape, abuse and female feticide, are real and have happened, and continue to take place, the characters and some of the places are fictitious and do not resemble any person living or dead. Any resemblance to any person is purely coincidental.

In June 2018 a global poll by Thomson Reuters Foundation ranked India as the most dangerous country in the world for women. India was ranked above Saudi Arabia, war-torn Afghanistan, Somalia and Syria. The six areas in which respondents were asked to rank the countries of the world were sexual and nonsexual violence, customary practices, access to economic resources and discrimination, healthcare and human trafficking.

The horrific rape of a young student in 2012 in Delhi followed by several other reported cases of rape of women and girls as young as five years in the recent past, as well as the horrific incident recently in Bihar demonstrate that not much has changed even though new laws were introduced. Tribal and religious practices and age old beliefs continue to keep women in the dark. According to Government data four cases of rape were reported every hour from 2007 to 2016.

"India has shown utter disregard and disrespect for women ... rape, marital rapes, sexual assault and harassment, female infanticide has gone unabated," said Manjunath Gangadhara, an official at the Karnataka state government,' is quoted in the report.

I Exist. Therefore I Am highlights some of these incidents through fictional characters and also talks about other instances of mistreatment that aren't discussed openly like the influence of caste, marriage, dowry, and the attitudes of family and society towards the other among us - women. No matter how educated, forward thinking, affluent or progressive she is, a woman will always be the other; the one to be used, exploited and thrown away once her purpose in life is served.

These then are the tales of the other in society; women from different walks of life, hailing from the metros and rural areas across the social and economic divide and age groups, facing diverse situation, always standing alone as society and family judge and condemn them. Their sole crime – being born female.

I hope the stories in this collection give you pause to think about the other and reach out to help women and girls subjected to abuse and exploitation find their way towards a future that is their right.

Shirani Rajapakse

Colombo, 2018

Drink Your Milk and Go to Sleep

There wasn't much I could do. It wasn't my decision, although I wish it was. Maaji, my mother-in-law ruled. There were other things to consider. A girl was just not right; we couldn't spend all that money on a girl. Besides, there was the dowry to think of and the marriage ceremony. Where would we find the money for all that?

The overpowering stench of rotting potatoes is around us. It is everywhere. It creeps into our hair, snuggles into our clothes, settles in the food we eat and enters our body with every breath we take. The disgusting odor is a reminder of the hardship of our lives here in the village. The last crop was lost. Again. There are debts to repay. The fields in front of me bear the scars of the loss. The stench is unbearable, but it is better than what is inside the house.

The branches of the gnarled old jamun tree sway gently in the breeze like an old woman fanning herself. The breeze strokes my face like a soft chiffon dupatta as if it is attempting to comfort me. It lifts the hairs come undone from the braid at the back and flicks them around towards my face where they move like a veil this way and that, now hiding now showing my eyes as if in jest. But there is nothing that can bring relief today, not even the breeze. I sit under the tree and wait. It is better than going inside. I will wait here for as long as I can, or as long as I'm allowed. No one will come to me now, at least not for a while. There are other more pressing things happening inside and I'm not required. They can take care of all that without me. My work is done, at least for now.

My friend Nalini lives in the house beyond the field. You can just catch a glimpse of it from where I am sitting if you look over the bushes at the side and through the opening between the two trees ahead. The smoke rises from the hearth in Nalini's house; blue gray wisps that try to form into a semblance of clouds but disappear on the breeze just as they rise over the branches of the sprawling trees that act like a cover over the house and property.

We both gave birth the same week three months ago. Was it really so long ago? Three months seems like an eternity when it really feels more like two weeks. I sit up with a start and count back to the day trying to see if I made a mistake in my tallying. But I'm not. It really was that long ago. I remember the day like it was this morning. The pain started in the night and we all thought it would happen soon, but it didn't. The darkness outside from the moonless night seemed to creep inside dulling the lamp in the corner and creating ominous shadows along the walls. The contractions went on for hours, growing more persistent until the soft cries broke the silence minutes before the roosters began to shake their feathers in preparation for their early morning call.

Two days later Nalini gave birth in the afternoon. There was no pain, no long drawn trepidation. She was happy. Ecstatic. The sun was shining brightly but it wasn't hot and sweltering like it had been earlier. It was a nice day to be out. The sun dappled leaves danced in the cool breeze and wafted into her house through open windows.

The difference is that Nalini is allowed to keep the child while I am not. I had to give up the child as it's not something the family wants. They expected something else, not that bawling bundle of feminine charm but a boy, virile and able to carry on the family name; someone that could work in the fields and earn a living. Not a girl. Dear God not a girl.

But you don't always get what you wish for. I was unlucky right from the start. The first time they found out it was a girl everyone was shocked. They had prayed so hard for a boy that when they got to know that it would be a girl they were bitterly disappointed. What could possibly have happened? Where had all those prayers gone? Maaji was so annoyed. However, there was nothing to be done. Fortunately the doctor was able to tell us what grew inside me before it was too late. He could get rid of the thing and send it back to where it came from. Everyone heaved a sigh of relief when they heard what the doctor did.

"Dear God, take this thing back and send us a boy instead," maaji cried out to God inside the mandir the next day.

But God, it seemed, didn't hear her. Or maybe her cries of despair were drowned by the jangling bells, or the drums beating outside. Or maybe He was just hard of hearing. Who was to know? Whatever the reason was it appeared as though I was destined to house baby girls inside my womb.

The second one too was detected early on as was the third. But the fourth was harder, almost as if she didn't want to leave. It took longer for the doctor to remove her and my insides screamed in protest. My clothes were soaked red and the table looked like a butcher had set up shop there. The pain churned inside me howling everywhere as if trying to find someplace to hide. A dark cloud of despair and helplessness hovered about. It enveloped me like a heavy blanket, similar to the kind we use during winter, pulling itself tighter every time I moved as if every action was tied to that one act that happened. It sneaked in and lodged in my heart. When it was all over even the doctor looked tired, although he had been doing things like this every day for as long as we could remember. The doctor was concerned as I had lost a lot of blood. He suggested I remain in the hospital for the rest of the day. But maaji wanted nothing of that.

"There is nothing wrong with her. My family has borne sons for generations and we have never rested. This girl is just making a fuss."

The doctor remained silent, but he was concerned. Before I left he told me to take it easy for a few days, no hard work, just relax. He also said I should wait for some time before trying again.

"She's too weak," the doctor said staring pointedly at maaji who sat next to me in his office.

But maaji merely harrumphed and walked out of the room muttering to herself not even bothering to wait for me. When we returned home she pounced on me accusing me of getting the doctor to speak on my behalf. My protests fell against silent walls and disappeared out of the windows at the sides. No one was interested. My husband turned away preferring to stare at the fields outside. He was bitterly disappointed. He thinks I should have borne him a son by now, but all I had managed to accomplish was lose the lives inside me. There must be something wrong with me.

But I didn't lose them; they were taken out of me. All of them.

He isn't interested in my logic.

"Your womb is diseased," maaji spat at me sitting on the corner of the charpoy that day.

I didn't reply, but looked down at my feet and tried to count my toes that seemed to shift this way and that like when you break the stillness of water to peer at what's beneath. When I lifted my hand to brush away the hair from my face it shook like an old woman's. All I wanted to do was curl up in a ball and let the pain melt away. But I couldn't; at least, not right then. They were all sitting there silently as if waiting for some miracle to take place.

"There are maggots inside you," maaji said staring daggers at me.

She let her eyes rest on each one of the family sitting in the room and raised her voice for effect.

"It's stuffed with maggots! Her womb is full of maggots!"

That was almost a year ago. The poojas increased. Every God we knew of was offered sweets and asked to intervene on our behalf. We begged and cajoled with prayers and offerings to placate their desires. We even visited a midwife in the next village who was famed for helping women with problems. She must be good because women from all over the land visited her to find solutions to their sorrows. She didn't talk much. There was no time for any words as it was obvious why we were all there. She had lots of customers like me waiting to be served every day. She gave me something to drink when I got home. The foul smell rushed out the moment I twisted the lid and I held my breath for as long as I could every time I swallowed the awful stuff that tasted like nothing I could even imagine. She said it would clear the space inside and make it clean and welcome for what was to come. I could barely eat as my stomach shuddered trying to get rid the horrible liquid churning inside. It's a good thing I became pregnant soon or I would not have known how to continue with no meals except that tablespoon of muck in the morning.

For the fifth time I returned to the doctor for the tests to check if everything was as we expected. This was the defining moment. A tired smile hovered at the corners of my lips after the doctor gave us the news. I was lucky. What relief. Things were going to be alright. I didn't have to go through all that pain again and no more remedies and strange things to eat or drink. No more strange acts to perform to appease the Gods. No more long arduous treks either to way out places to visit this or that person famed with helping women like me. Life was better at home too. Maaji stopped her incessant moaning about me. I didn't have to listen to all those negative thoughts anymore. That was such a load off my shoulders. Our prayers were finally answered. At last. All those poojas to the Gods were not in vain. I had a gift from God.

Life was good until that moment three months ago. It was almost as if all that ugliness that had followed me had vanished somewhere and happiness had approach to engulf me. I was with my mother in my old home when I gave birth. I felt like the old me all over again, carefree and happy. It was a joyous occasion. We could laugh and joke about trivial things, unlike during the past occasions. God was on our side. Even maaji's face had softened when I walked out of the door to return to my mother's home for the birth.

"Come back soon with our gift," she said exposing a toothy grin I had never seen in all the time I had been in that house.

The friendly, familiar faces around me eased the pain through the long hours into the night. My sister and mother took turns to sit with me, chanting slokas and singing to me to ease the pain. They talked to me recounting old memories and stories I remembered from my youth and occasionally cracking jokes. The soft smell of jasmine permeated the air from the incense burner outside the room. As the pain progressed my mother went to the kitchen to boil water and get something for me to drink while my sister sat next to me and sang softly until the new sounds took over, soft yet strong. The little cries that told me everything was going to be fine. I smiled when I heard the little voice mingling with the soft notes from my sister's song.

Then they both stopped abruptly. When I turned to my sister she refused to look at me but busied herself with tidying the place. There was a sudden hushed silence. I was too exhausted to ask what was bothering them until the midwife came towards me her lips pursed and roughly shoved a pink bundle into my arms. She then left the room. I looked down at the little girl in my arms. How could this be? My mother averted her eyes as I sought hers in confusion. What had happened? They had all promised me a boy. The doctor had not said anything was wrong, and the midwife had assured everything would be fine. But here I was holding a baby girl in my arms.

When the news reached my husband's house maaji had wailed in anguish. It was as if a close relative had died. When I returned to my husband's home a few weeks later carrying the little bundle they welcomed me with a dirge. The celebrations were tinged with sadness and the impeding gloom that would soon follow. But no one spoke about it. There was a silent understanding that it wasn't to be spoken about; there was no need to voice the inevitable. Everyone knew like they knew that the night turned to day that what was to follow would follow. They just had to set a date.

I remember the joy with the newborn. We didn't give her a name. It would be of no use as she wouldn't need it. God would give her a name when she got there. But I gave her a name. I called my daughter Pooja, the offering that had come to me, and the offering I would soon make to God.

"Pooja," I whispered into her ear when no one was around.

I took care of her amidst the chores of the house. There was barely any time to rest or spend time with her even when she was crying out in hunger. Maaji wasn't interested.

"Save your milk for the sons you will produce," she screamed when she saw me rushing to feed Pooja.

But I couldn't ignore the cries of the helpless child. My husband didn't grudge me either. He too seemed happy to see the child and I hoped he would stand up for the little thing when the time came. I hoped he would reason with his mother. But I was wrong. Very wrong.

❀

The bottle of pesticides is on the floor under the bed where I left it. There is still a lot remaining inside. I only used a little. That was enough. The deed was done.

"Drink your milk and go to sleep." I whispered into her ear as I held her tightly to my breast for the last time.

Silent tears fell on her face as she gagged on the strange fluid and then she went limp. I held her for as long as I could then I left her there in the room, swaddled in blankets to keep her warm like I always did. But the child had gone cold and no amount of warmth from the blankets could make her feel again. Her tiny hands stuck out to the heavens as if imploring all the Gods to intervene in the act. But the Gods kept away; perhaps they too were shocked at the callous ways of the people. None came to save the child. Her pale skin turned blue black. There was immense anguish written in the expression of her tiny face as if that final act was too much for her to stand.

I came outside to wait. There is nothing else to do. It is always quiet here under the jamun tree at the back of the house. No one comes to disturb me. I can't bear to look at the child like that. It isn't right, but there is nothing much I can do. If only the potatoes were saved?

There won't be any chores for me today. I am allowed to moan the loss at least for the day. I will sit here under the jamun tree until I can sit no more. The others are preparing the front room, spreading cloth on the floor for the guests to sit. I will join them later with the women of the family. My mother and sisters have not arrived as yet. Neither have the neighbors. There is time yet. The holy man is expected later on. Soon the house will be full of people, talking, eating and reciting slokas.

We are sending back the gift from God and asking Him to send another in its place. A different type; a boy. God can keep the girl as His helper. She can clean the place and help keep it neat and tidy. There is more work waiting for her there in His house. She isn't needed here. She can be spared. The holy man will double the efforts to ask God to send a boy soon.

After that the men in the family will take her with them. They will leave her in the place they leave everyone that is waiting to meet God and then they will return. The women will remain inside the house and will leave later. When there is nothing more to eat and no more conversations to make.

I stare into the distance. Nalini's family is making preparations for the naming ceremony. It will take place in a few days from now. I will not attend that ceremony. I had my own ceremony for my daughter in private. No one knew about it except the two of us and of course, God. But now only I know. It doesn't matter anymore.

The smoke rises from the hearth in Nalini's house. I watch it rise up, up trying valiantly to reach the sky and mingle with the clouds passing by. Soon another fire will be lit and an offering made to God. The smoke from that fire will rise up in the sky and reach out to the heavens. I stare unseeing in front of me as a sudden deluge floods my eyes flowing out unabated, silent and forceful like the stream at the other end of the village that flows fast and silent, carrying the melted snow from the mountains beyond.

Shweta's Journey

Shweta pushed back a strand of hair that fell across her forehead with the back of her hand. The water from her fingers fell on her hair flattening the wayward strands against her head. She sat back on her haunches and sighed heavily. Washing clothes was a tough job, much harder than she had ever imagined. She was accustomed to throwing her clothes into the washing machine back in her flat, pressing a few buttons and leaving the clothes there until it was time to take them out again. The clothes would wash themselves clean and wring themselves of all excess water. All she had to do was take them out of the machine and hang them to dry in the sun on the clothes line strung across the large balcony outside. That was how clothes were washed in the city. That was how she knew it to be.

When she was small and washing machines were a thing of the future, a dhobi came home to do the washing. Shweta sat on the little wooden stool in their small family garden and intently observed as the dhobi washed all the clothes. The dhobi carried the soiled clothes and placed them inside the big basin under the tap at the clothes washing area near the kitchen. She opened the tap and let the water flow in to soak the clothes. Once the basin was full and the clothes were soaked she picked up the items, one by one. Placing them on the cement floor, she squatted in front and began vigorously rubbing soap into them. When all were soaped and collected on a pile at the side she picked up a few, folded them to a certain size and holding them by the edges she started beating them against the hard floor. Thuk, thuk, thuk went the clothes as they hammered against the floor.

Shweta loved to listen to the crash of the clothes pounding against the ground. She would sit close to the dhobi and stare as she lifted up items of clothing in an arch above her head and bring them down hard onto the floor. Splat! She lifted them up again and again and brought them down again and again. It was like watching a machine work round and round as the clothes flew in a circle, up in the air and then thrash itself on the floor and up again. Mesmerized she gazed at the movement of clothes held tightly in the dhobis hand lifting up as she drew her arm up and as far back as she could then brought it down hard on the ground and back up and down again many times. Little drops of water and soap suds flew in the air as the clothes made an arc upwards and down. Shweta listened to the sound as she watched the arm of the dhobi work its way with each item of clothing. Sometimes she counted the number of times each item of clothing was beaten against the floor; sometimes she just watched and listened, enthralled by the scene in front of her.

No one in her family washed clothes. It was not something they did. There were others to do it for them. Shweta had never washed clothes, although she had seen the dhobi wash clothes many, many times and she knew how it was done.

Shweta smiled to herself as she recollected the memory yet a troubled look entered her eyes. What would her family say if they saw her like this now? She wondered feeling a little sad and ashamed of herself. But she quickly brushed away those thoughts of her life before her mind began to start wondering about things best left unsaid. Shweta sighed and returned to her washing. She picked up Swamiji's silk trouser and slowly began rubbing soap into it.

Swamiji had returned the previous day from a long overdue journey to America. He had gone there on the invitation of several of his devout disciples. They had pleaded with him to come to America to talk to them, and teach them about the Gods and about meditation. They also wanted him to conduct classes for the younger generation and instruct them about the Gods in the old country. Not having much influence in their lives in the new country many of the youngsters knew little to nothing about the old ways and the rituals and practices, so it would be good for them to spend some time to learn about their history and where they came from. But Swamiji had been unable to fulfill their requests as the time just wasn't right. He couldn't give his full concentration to the task with so much still undecided back at home so he put off the journey to America for a long time until he felt settled enough in his mind to make the move. His two elder sons had finished college and were to be married and he needed to be there for them. But now with those responsibilities taken care of, Swamiji decided it was time to take up the offer of travel. It would be good to spread his wings and meet new people he said.

Shweta hadn't accompanied Swamiji to America as his devotees only sent one ticket for him and Shweta didn't have the money to buy herself a ticket. Although she too knew a lot about religion they were more interested in hearing from Swamiji. They informed that they would be happy to have her too and would make arrangements for her stay, but they were unable to pay her air ticket at that moment.

"If someone can pay your return ticket..." they left the rest unsaid and Shweta had smiled sadly and nodded. She had looked away knowing that voicing her wish would not get her anywhere.

ॐ

Shweta handed over all her money to Swamiji when they married. She also gave her jewelry; her grandmothers' heavy diamond studded gold ornaments as well as a few other pieces. He affirmed that she would not need any jewelry anymore as she was now leading a religious life and such worldly pleasures were of no use. They were a sign of ostentation; of decadence. She need not wear any adornments except the simple sandalwood bead chain. She was married to a Swami and was on her way to moksha. There was no need of showiness anymore. Her love and devotion to God was the only adornment she would need. Swamiji insisted that she give up everything worldly if she wanted to achieve her stated objective. At first Shweta had protested.

"My mother will be upset," she said referring to her grandmother's ornaments.

They rightfully belonged to her family and Shweta was reluctant to sell them. She wanted to return them all to her mother and sister, along with the money she had earned that was in her bank account. Swamiji had been annoyed. Very annoyed.

"How can you even think of it?" he demanded angrily.

He paced the room like a caged tiger as she sat shivering on her mat in the corner unsure what to say or do.

Up and down, up and down he paced his stride forceful and firm. He glared at her as he passed mumbling words she didn't hear. She was so afraid that it was as if she had blocked out all sounds except the stride of his footsteps moving across the room and the angry slap, slap of his new chappals on the tiled floor.

"Jewelry and money are evils that take you further away from God," he said loudly, stopping his pacing to stare at her trembling on her mat.

"Yes, Swamiji," she croaked out in fear. "That was why I thought I'd return it to my mother," she added looking hopeful, but Swamiji's voice thundered, every syllable echoing across the walls in the small room.

"ENOUGH!" he roared lifting his hand up to his shoulder, his palm facing out. "Enough of this nonsense!" he bellowed and Shweta cowered low as if to prevent the words from flattening her to the ground. He stood there looking down at her, his eyes blazing, a stern look on his face.

"You don't need them and neither does your mother. Or your sister. Or your brother. Or anyone else."

Shweta whimpered in response. She would have said and done anything to stop him. Anything. But she was paralyzed with fear and couldn't speak or even move. She acquiesced without any further ado and handed over everything to him. She didn't even tell her mother about it as she knew her mother would be horrified at what she had done. She didn't know what happened to the jewelry or the money that she withdrew from the bank the next day, and didn't dare ask. She no longer had the right to ask, or so he made her believe, so she kept quiet and didn't question him.

Shweta wasn't really married to him. Not in the real sense. There was no huge marriage ceremony attended by family and friends that went on for days like most marriage ceremonies everyone was accustomed to. There was no mehendi ceremony either. No pretty clothes and jewelry and no announcement to the community that she was now a married woman. People were curious about their relationship. They were also concerned and they sometimes voiced it to him, telling him in no uncertain terms that it wasn't fair to Shweta as she was a young girl and should rightfully be married and having a family. After a while he decided to make their relationship official in order to stop the questioning and the comments passed by people they frequently met. He surprised her in Varanasi when they went to meet Swamiji's guru who had come from the Himalayas to spend some time in the city of the Gods. They had walked around the sacred fire in Varanasi and he had placed vermillion on the parting of her hair to pronounce her status as his wife.

But she wasn't really his wife.

Swamiji was still married to Mina his first wife. There was nothing written down to say they were married to each other, but their respective families knew they were married. Virendra Singh had married Mina twenty nine years ago. They never divorced as it was unheard of in their circles. They had merely moved apart.

When Virendra retired from his job their youngest son was in his final year at school. Virendra found himself with nothing to do. Life stretched out in front of him in a never ending line of boredom. Virendra was accustomed to living it up; parties and get-togethers with their mutual friends almost twice a week, tennis on Sundays followed by a leisurely lunch at the club and many other events to keep him busy and occupied. But this all changed at retirement. Virendra wasn't able to sustain his lavish lifestyle with his pension. This made him extremely frustrated and moody. He didn't want to take up a job somewhere else either and had been brooding for a while when the thought hit him in the face. There were many people that were seeking spiritual satisfaction. The large number of foreigners who were living in the city having come for work and other reasons were curious to learn about Hinduism and were seeking out various religious leaders and swamis.

Virendra had been slightly amused at their naïve questions when he met some of them at one or other of the never ending cocktail parties he attended. He was amazed as there were many locals that were also looking for holy men to guide them on their journey towards moksha. Virendra had even directed them to some religious leader or the other that would teach them about the way to moksha. But the problem was that most swamis in the country didn't know English and this was a real setback for the non Hindi speakers. Virendra had some training in religion and he was well read on the subject. He spent hours explaining to most of the crowd that hung eagerly onto his words like they did to their cocktails.

After some rigorous training with a well known guru that lived in the foothills of the Himalayas Virendra decided that the time was right for him too to begin working for the Gods. With gurujis blessings Virendra changed his name to Swami Ramakrishna. He had been away for so long, almost three months that his circle of friends and acquaintances began to wonder what had become of him. When Virendra arrived one evening at a cocktail party and announced that he had become a Swami and was now going to conduct classes they all believed and applauded him.

"What a brilliant idea," Sonia gushed, almost spilling her cocktail as she rushed towards him to plant loud kisses on his cheeks. "I wish you all the best," she cooed as others crowded around him.

"You are just the person for it," Mamata said.

"Now we can all reach moksha faster because we have a real swami amongst us," Primrose said smiling at him.

Shweta had moved to the city a few months back and was just beginning to make friends. She smiled as she sipped her cocktail. "You should have a retreat for all of us," she said earnestly.

"Yes, why not? You can start at my home. The doors are wide open to you," Sonia said with a flourish of her arms to indicate her largesse.

Swami Ramakrishna was delighted by the reaction. He was even more pleased by the number of people that attended his first retreat. Not only was he able to bring in a lot of people and guide them towards God, but he also made a lot of money. He had by then separated from Mina claiming he needed to be alone. His spiritual journey required that he remain single, he told her assuring her that he would nevertheless do his duty by his children and see that they got married and settle down in life.

He moved into a house in one of the posh areas of town that was donated to him by a well wisher and he felt happy with the way things were moving. He had nothing to worry about as all his needs were fulfilled. He even had a woman who came in twice a week to do the housework; clean, sweep, do the grocery shopping and cook for him. She cooked enough food for him to keep in the fridge and eat on the days she didn't come in to work.

Swamiji didn't like to eat frozen food. He really didn't want to take out precooked food that was a day old that he had to then heat before eating. It didn't taste the same. He was accustomed to eating warm food cooked minutes before it was consumed and this new eating style was unpalatable. He missed Mina's cooking, but there was nothing he could do. He didn't say anything as the food and the cooks' wages were all paid for by his disciples. He would wait until the right time to mention that the woman should come in everyday to cook and clean. He would wait patiently he told himself. Until then he continued as usual making a face every time he put a spoonful of the day old preheated food in his mouth. But he didn't grumble or complain to anyone.

That was a month ago.

Swamiji got out of the car and gawked at the building in front of him. It was a fairly large house that seemed to have been constructed in a haphazard manner, as if the inhabitants had hurried put it together and then found they hadn't enough space and had added more parts to it. There was no coherent shape to the house. Things jutted out at odd places. It was a strange house he mused as he pocked his car keys and slowly walked up the long driveway towards the front door.

The house belonged to Mamata, one of his newest disciples. She was living on one side with her husband and their old parents in that strange house that belonged to her husband's family. The other side belonged to her brother-in-law. But they all used the same front door that now opened wide as he approached. Mamata came out to stand at the side, beaming at him as he walked up, her arms folded in reverence. Sonia was unable to organize the retreat at her house like she did the first time as her mother-in-law had suddenly been taken ill and it would have been difficult to organize a retreat there. She was worried and had almost been in tears at the thought of letting Swamiji down so soon but Mamata had come to her rescue immediately.

Mamata was dressed in a beautiful white saree with a bright red border running on both sides to meet at the end in the same red with a design in gold woven through the red. She had a large round vermillion dot right in the middle of her forehead and she was wearing her usual diamond ear rings and pendant. So indiscreet, yet so stylish, he noted with satisfaction. He wondered how many people were inside, waiting for his arrival as he sauntered over towards her.

"Mamataji, you look ravishing, as usual!" he exclaimed bending his head slightly towards her as he touched her folded hands.

Mamata threw back her head and laughed. It sounded like the tinkling of bells in the mandir.

"You are always complementing me," she said as she turned around and walked inside the house her wide hips sashaying to the beat of the little bells in her anklets, beckoning him to follow.

The living room was packed with people, mostly women, dressed in white sarees, all expensive silks like Mamata's that crackled softly as they moved. They rose from their seats and bowed their heads in greeting as they brought their hands together in front of them. Swamiji mimicked the gesture as he smiled to everyone around the room. He moved towards the seat on the dais that had been prepared for him. He continued to smile as his eye took in the group of women who sat down and gazed at him compassionately waiting expectantly for the gems of wisdom they hoped he would bestow on them.

Shweta was sitting between two older women towards the left. She was staring at him with rapt adoration in her eyes. Swamiji smiled warmly at her and her face took on a look of pure unadulterated reverence, as if the smile itself was enough to lift her to moksha. Swamiji had met Shweta at the first pooja at Sonia's and again at another held at the house of another one of his affluent disciples living in the city. Shweta had completed her studies at the university two years ago and was working for a new NGO for the downtrodden when they met. She was full of zest for life and everyone who had heard about her said that she had a very bright future ahead of her. She was placed in charge of several projects run by the NGO purely because of her efficiency and competency. She had gone abroad for several conferences and presented papers. She was the talk of the town and everyone was thrilled if she made it even for a few minutes to their parties. They were all predicting great things for her.

Shweta never imagined she would marry Swamiji or anyone like him. He was old enough to be her grandfather and not someone she would have been attracted to. He just wasn't her type. But something had happened during one of those weekly religious meetings they held at Sonia's place. Shweta had also attended one of the week long retreats and it was after the retreat that she had decided to give up her life and all worldly pleasures to serve Swamiji. Shweta remembered the dismay on the faces of her colleagues at work when she said she would no longer work for them, but had decided to work for Swamiji instead.

"You don't need to give up your job to do Gods work," Shankar said with concern."Besides, working for the downtrodden, trying to better their lives is also God's work."

"Why would you want to give up all this?" Reena asked puzzled.

Shweta was the head of one unit at the NGO. She had a doctorate in social science and was the most sought after speaker on women's rights. She had a very bright future ahead of her. Everyone was surprised and a little worried about the sudden change of plans in her life. But Shweta was adamant. She smiled and didn't say anything more. A week after announcing her decision she moved into the small room at the back of Swamijis house. The whole place was a mess and Shweta was shocked into silence. Even the slums she visited regularly were cleaner. The woman who came to do the housework for Swamiji either didn't know what to do or she didn't do anything. Besides the woman didn't come every day and was somewhat irregular.

"Why don't you take over," Swamiji suggested smiling warmly at her when she questioned him about the state of the place.

The woman was dismissed and Shweta took up the work without a word of protest. Her friends began to worry about her, thinking she was being forced to do the work by Swamiji. They admonished him whenever they met him, but it didn't seem to help. He merely smiled and said that it was her idea.

"She decided to do the work," he said, "the woman didn't come one day and Shweta here was so upset that I wouldn't get any food that she went to the kitchen and started cooking," he said looking around as if to make sure everyone was listening to him. "Arre, you should have seen her. She was like a real tornado. All angry and cursing the woman for not coming in. I was quite scared yaar," he said trying to make light of it. "I never thought she could get so angry. She is so mild and timid. I was surprised," he said and dismissed any more questions about the incident.

But they were worried for her. They tried to reason with her.

"It's alright to do the cooking, but the washing and cleaning? You are not a dhobi," Mamata said emphatically.

"Yaar, Shwetaji, why do you work like a slave for that old man. He has grownup sons and a wife. They can take care of him," Nandini added.

They urged her to find someone to do the work. But all they achieved was to isolate Shweta further. The more they questioned her out of concern the more she moved away from them withdrawing silently and hiding from everyone she knew. Shweta distanced herself from them all, her friends, colleagues and even her own flesh and blood. She locked herself up inside an invisible shell she seemed to have covered herself with. She didn't attend the cocktail parties or dinners or other get-togethers organized by her friends and colleagues. She also stopped attending the theatre, something she had enjoyed so much. And there were other changes too. Visible changes.

Shweta altered her wardrobe as well. Gone were the expensive chiffon embroidered sarees and silk kurtas that she so loved to wear. Shweta stared to dress in badly tailored kurtas in homespun cottons she bought at the shop in the market. She exchanged her stilettos for coarse leather chappals. She stopped straightening her shoulder length hair and began letting it grow long and wild. She even stopped wearing makeup. The only adornment she wore was the small vermillion bindi on her forehead and later the line of vermillion in the parting of her hair to indicate her status as a married woman. Shweta still looked the same, but there was a washed out look about her that people found very distressing.

Shweta toiled hard in the house plus attended to Swamiji's religious work. She claimed she was pleased to be serving Swamiji as it was like serving God. She was also glad to be married to Swamiji as she now had status in society and people, especially the neighbors didn't look at her with derision. But her friends knew something was not quite right. They even began to feel slightly disgusted with Swamiji. There was no need for Shweta to give up everything she had achieved in order to reach moksha. She could do this without becoming a religious slave. Swamiji could have hired someone to do his work instead of forcing Shweta. They felt she was being unfairly treated, but none of them could say anything to her. He was always there when they spoke to her, hovering about like a dark cloud about to burst. Swamiji listened to them and then rudely brushed aside their words. He insisted that it was Shweta's decision to come live in his house. It was her decision alone and he had nothing to do with it, he bellowed out in annoyance.

"Did I force you to come and work for me?" he turned towards Shweta and asked her somewhat gruffly.

"No," Shweta said meekly looking down at her hands, "It was my decision."

He stared hard at her and she squirmed on the rough cushion she was sitting on. She couldn't look into his eyes and neither did she want to look at the people who were around her. She felt so ashamed and lost.

She looked down and away and avoided eye contact. It seemed so unlike her, yet no one could say anything. The Shweta they knew would never have agreed to something like this. The feisty woman who had taken a stand for other women was now reduced to insignificance. She who had traveled to many remote areas encouraging women to assert their rights appeared to have turned into a meek frail woman who didn't seem capable of standing up for her own rights. They were saddened. But what they didn't know was that in her heart Shweta too was miserable. Yet there was nothing she could do about it. There was some force stronger than she could control that was making her do things this way. She sighed to herself and smiled wanly at her friends without really looking at anyone lest she see things in their faces she didn't want to.

It was after the confrontation at his house with her friends that Swamiji took her to Varanasi where they were married. No one was present at the ceremony. They had to take Shweta's word for it. No one could do anything about it. Her friends and family didn't come to visit her at the house either. Swamiji explained to them that Shweta had undertaken a huge task; she was using every minute of the day she had to learn all she could about God and the way to reach him. Swamiji asked them not to disturb her as she was practicing her religion very diligently. She had specific times to study the religious texts and times for meditation.

Of course they could visit, he said smiling, but this had to be limited to the evenings when they conducted poojas at the house thrice a week. Yet there was no time during these visits to sit down and talk with Shweta as she was busy. She looked the same, yet there were lines on her face. There were streaks of premature gray in her long hair that she now wore in an untidy braid at the back of her head. The skin on her arms and legs were stretched and dry like a workers and not someone that had lived in comfort. Her nails were chapped and discolored and she looked like an old woman. They stared at her and wondered at the futility of studying religion. If this was what religion did to someone that was so full of life and as intelligent and brilliant as Shweta, then what would it do to them, they wondered.

"I don't think this is right," Nandini whispered as they left the house after one of the poojas.

"Yes, religion doesn't turn people into slaves," Bina added slowly, "Just look what has become of her? She even dresses worse than my maid."

"I heard she gave all her money and jewelry to Swamiji," Shankar said. "Someone down the road said he saw Swamiji selling her sarees and other things."

The two girls stopped and stared at him aghast.

"What?" Bina exclaimed in horror.

"Why would she give him all her money? What would she live on?" Nandini asked.

"Maybe that's why she is like that. She has nothing left," Shankar said after a while.

"Can't we get her out of there?" Nandini asked.

"We can't. She won't come. You saw the way she said she was staying there on her own free will. It would be hard for anyone to get her to leave," Mamata said joining them to stand outside the gate and talk.

"What if we inform the police?" Nandini asked.

"Won't be of much use as they won't be able to do a thing. She will say she is there because she wants to be," Mamata added.

"Swamiji will make her say she is there on her own free will," Shankar corrected.

Mamata nodded but didn't say anything. They walked slowly down the road towards their cars parked some distance away lost in thought.

They didn't attend the pooja the next time and slowly they all began dropping off completely, making some excuse or the other not to attend the poojas. There was disgust with Swamiji for what he was doing to Shweta and they had no desire to learn about religion from him. After some time none of the old crowd attended the poojas. Sonia didn't offer her place for anymore retreats either making some excuse or

34

the other about the non availability of the place. Reena too was disgusted and asked him to leave the house as she needed it for some relatives that were visiting. None of them wanted anything to do with him anymore. They were also afraid of what he would do to them or the friends they would introduce to him. But there was no shortage of disciples. For every person that left Swamiji seemed to attract another two. Someone offered him a house to live on the other side of town and he moved in immediately.

Shweta's eyes began to tear as she remembered her friends concern during those early days. She had wanted more than anything to say she craved to leave, but something had changed her words. What had come out of her mouth was something completely different to the words she had formed inside her head. She was as startled at what she said when she said it, but there was nothing she could do. It was as if she had no control of her words, just as she had no control of her body or her life. Yet she still had some control over her thoughts and this was what made her sad. She yearned to return to her life that she had left, but she was hemmed in tight. She couldn't speak out now either. It would not be right. He had agreed to marry her and had given the respect due to her. He was her husband now. She sighed heavily, blinked away the tears and began to scrub Swamijis dirty clothes.

A Room Full of Horrors

It was like leaving a war zone to enter a vacuum. Not a whisper, a sigh or even the sound of breathing. If someone had dropped a pin you would probably have heard it turn over several times on the cement floor before it stretched itself flat, settling on its side to wait for what would happen next. The sound would have echoed so loud you'd have heard it magnified several times. It was truly an eerie silence that settled in the room at the far end of the corridor as the girls stepped inside laughing, recollecting the incident about Arun's hair. They didn't notice the effect their entry created on the people in that small room. Everyone was pretending to work. They were all staring into their big dusty ledgers, yet it was obvious to any outsider who was not part of that working environment that their minds were not on the figures in those ledgers. The usually noisy room had suddenly lost its voice.

Mr. Singh appeared flustered. He was in the process of shouting at someone that came in to clear up some details, but stopped short on seeing the girls at the door. In fact he was stopped short in mid sentence, his mouth half forming the next word yet unable to utter the sound, his arms suspended in the air, somewhere between the table and his head. The expression on his face soon changed. Gone was the look of annoyance to be replaced with a foolish grin. Yet his brain didn't appear to have given him any signals as his arms remained suspended in mid air.

Everyone inside the room resumed their composure and continued with their work, as if nothing had happened, though part of their being was attuned to the movements of the two girls entering the room. The other students that came to get their work done looked annoyingly at them. Foreign students. Why such an interest in foreign students? They wondered in distaste, even a little annoyance as they glanced at the girls standing hesitantly near the door.

"Forr-rin students, yaar" a loud whisper from the fat woman in the far corner confirmed what all of them already knew.

What was wrong with these people? The girls approached the now grinning and wildly gesturing Mr. Singh. This was now almost like a routine for them. The first time they had come on their own, not together, and didn't notice the effect they created. Besides, they were made to run here, there and everywhere, getting signatures onto pieces of paper even from people they thought had no earthly reason to put their signatures on any paper. They had no choice but take the papers around the Administrative Block and across to the lecture halls to get the professors signatures. The next time they went together. At least they could keep each other company, trudging around the campus for signatures and then dropping the completed forms at the prescribed places. It was almost like some weird paper relay.

They had been disgusted with Mr. Singh's demeanor that first time they encountered him. He'd salivated like a dog after a long chase in the hot sun. The sight was quite revolting to say the least. Yet they couldn't get away as they had to wait and watch. Stay and observe Mr. Singh suck in his cheeks as he counted the notes of money one by one. He giggled like a young boy that just exchanged his first words of romance with a girl, much less a kiss. That would come later. Much later and may have been just as clumsy. He probably giggled helplessly for anything out of the ordinary. Days like today were certainly out of the ordinary.

"Sit down, sit down," he grinned his much too toothy grin, jumping out of his seat to pull another chair from the corner as they approached his desk. "So, how is your country? You went home for holiday?" he demanded settling back into his chair and crossing his hands in front of his chest.

"No we didn't go home. We stayed here," Karen spoke for them both.

"Why you didn't go home?" demanded Mr. Singh, a look of surprise on his already grinning face.

"We can't afford to go home every holiday. It's very expensive. We're students," Iris explained.

"You can't afford it!" Mr. Singh almost choked. "You can't afford it!" he spat out and started to laugh, tears coming into his eyes. "You take a flight back home. Ask your parents to send you the ticket," he said in between laughs.

"The return ticket costs too much. Besides it makes no sense to spend so much money to fly home just for a few weeks," Iris forced herself to be patient.

However no sooner had she finished her sentence than Mr. Singh bellowed.

"But you are forr-rin students. You are rich. You CAN afford it!"

"Even if we can or can't, how would you know?" Karen demanded getting quite angry with the charade.

"But you are forr-rin students"...

A glare from both the girls shut him up. Mr. Singh composed himself. His silly grin was back on his face.

"So what can I do for you today?" he asked, slapping his hands together on the table and looking around at his colleagues around the room. They were now quite openly enjoying the conversation at Mr. Singh's table and had stopped their work to take in the entertainment.

"Maa-dam, what is the prrarb-lem?" Mr. Singh shouted out at no one in particular. "Bring that paper here. Yes, yes, what's the prrarb-lem?" he demanded beckoning to a student who was trying to make the clerk at one of the tables at the back understand something.

But of course the clerks' mind was not on his work that day. The student strode towards Mr. Singh with the paper thankful that someone wanted to take some notice.

"Show it to him," said Mr. Singh with a casual glance at the paper the student was trying vainly to thrust into his face, waving him in the direction of another clerk.

"We came to pay our fees. Can we pay it NOW?" Karen demanded before he could find some other distraction.

"You want to pay your fees. Why come here? Go pay to cashier saab. There's a queue outside. Go in to queue. Go, go," he said authoritatively, the grin still plastered across his face, though a look of undisguised revulsion was now mixed in.

"But we have to pay to you. You said so the last time," Karen all but spat out.

"No I didn't say that. I'm not cashier. Why you pay to me? You go pay to cashier," he said pointing angrily in the direction of the cashier.

"Go. Go," he almost shouted.

"You told us. The cashier told us. We have to give the money to you as we're foreign students," Karen shouted back.

"Aaah, forr-rin students," crooned Mr. Singh silkily. "You pay dollars? American dollars?" he demanded. "You give me six hundred dollars," he said sticking his right hand out to receive the money.

"No, we don't pay in dollars. We pay in rupees."

His face fell.

"Indian rupees?" he demanded foolishly.

"Why, will you accept American rupees?" Iris retorted in disgust.

"Hahahaha. There are no American rupees. This is good joke yaar. Very good joke," he said shaking with laughter. "Wait, let me see. You have to pay thirty three thousand six hundred rupees and twenty cents. Indian rupees," he said converting the rate on a piece of dirty scrap paper.

"But you are converting at yesterday's rate. You should convert at today's rate."

Iris looked annoyed. She glared at him. Karen nodded her head.

"No today's rate. No today's rate," he retorted, in spite of it now being almost noon.

Iris glanced at her watch which read ten minutes past eleven. She sighed.

"Look at the paper. You'll find today's rate in it," Karen said.

"Where's today's paper. Give me today's paper," he barked angrily.

"What, do you expect us to being our fees with a newspaper for you? Don't you have a newspaper here? You should know what the rate is, or if you don't, then read a paper. Today's paper," Iris shot back angrily.

"I know the rate. It's yesterday's rate. Today's rate is the same as yesterday's rate," Mr. Singh was by now screaming. "Where's the paper? Bring me today's paper," he bellowed at one of the many peons who ran out and returned immediately with a rather crumpled newspaper.

Mr. Singh grabbed the newspaper and started shuffling through the pages till he came to the page on which the days' foreign exchange rates were printed. One glance was enough.

"Today's rate is same as yesterday's rate," he slammed the paper down.

"Of course it is. If you look at yesterday's paper," Karen said wearily.

Mr. Singh's mouth fell open. It took him quite a while to snap out of that pose. His face had by now turned dark pink. He glared at the dateline at the top of the page. It was yesterday's date. He transferred his glare to the peon sitting at a table a little distance away. The peon was of course happily taking all this in, enjoying himself thoroughly oblivious to the embarrassment he'd caused Mr. Singh.

"Then you will pay at yesterday's rate," Mr. Singh screamed, the dark pink on his face turning to purple. "Here! This is the rate."

He threw the piece of paper on which he had converted the rate to rupees at them. The paper landed on the ground with the force of it.

"Pay that now or get out of here," he yelled and leaned back in his chair.

"Whaat is the prrarb-lem Singhji?" the fat woman from the far corner waddled over, puffed up for a fight like an overstuffed turkey.

"Kutch nahin, maadam," Mr. Singh feigned weariness.

Upon hearing the weariness in his voice the woman pounced on the girls.

"Why you bar-thering Mr. Singh? He's a heart patient. You shouldn't trraa-ble him yaar," she scolded. "We are very busy people. Pay your fees and get out," she shouted, her shrill voice rising to a feverish pitch.

"Shut up!" both girls retorted in unison.

"Go sit in your corner and mind your own business," Karen added and glared at the woman.

The effect was amazing. The woman looked visibly deflated. It was as though someone had opened the valve for the air to burst out of her. She hovered around for a while, lost for words, looking at the money being counted out by the girls.

"If you are such a busy person why do you come here? Go back and attend to your work. Go." Karen said firmly before the woman could open her mouth and say anything else.

"But beti, I'm trying to help only. Whaat is the prrarb-lem. Tell me, beti," she suddenly gushed as if she was bestowed with the talent of solving the world's problems.

"If you want to help go away and mind your own business."

The woman stared. Openmouthed. Stunned. She glanced at the girls, at Mr. Singh and then back at the girls. One glare from them both and she shut up and waddled off to her place.

"Here's the money," Karen handed over the amount to Mr. Singh.

"Count it," he said in an uninterested manner.

"You count it. Now," Iris said. She was quite fed up with this tirade that they had to go over each time they came to pay their fees.

"Why does it always have to be like this? Why do we always have to go through this?" she murmured through her teeth, but Karen only sighed in response.

She too was weary of the whole charade and was wishing she had never stepped foot in the place. Mr. Singh pulled the bundle of tightly stapled 100 rupee notes towards him. He wet his finger on his tongue and started leafing through the notes.

"Hundred, two hundred, three hundred"... he droned on moistening his finger on his tongue frequently.

There was silence in the room. All eyes were turned towards the counting of Mr. Singh. The peon sitting at the other end of the room sauntered towards the table next to Mr. Singh and perched on the edge of a chair. His eyes never strayed from the bundle of notes.

"Why you give torn money?" interrupted Mr. Singh, breaking the monotony of his counting. "I can't accept torn notes."

He glanced up from his counting, the silly grin back on his face.

"Do you expect us to print new notes for you?" Iris demanded.

"It's your money. Your bank. If that's how you treat your money, don't expect us to blame for it. Now count," Karen snapped at him.

Mr. Singh resumed his counting, the silly grin now a permanent fixture on his face.

"Right. Correct," he said glancing up. "You are also paying today?" he asked innocently, looking at Iris.

She gave him a dirty look and took out several bundles of neatly folded hundred rupee notes from her bag.

She had withdrawn the money on two occasions and didn't have it stapled up into bundles of five thousands or ten thousands like Karen. She counted them out into little bundles of thousands and placed them on the table in front of Mr. Singh. He started to drool as she began counting the bundles and placing them neatly one next to the other. He was mesmerized by the sight of the notes. His eyes followed Iris's hands as she counted and arranged the bundles on the table. He was by now in a sheer state of drool. The bundles were neatly piled in front of him.

"That's all?"

He looked at her, a hint of disappointment entering his voice as he realized she had stopped adding any more bundles of money to the pile. Neither of the girls offered any comment. He silently began to count the money, going through the same routine of wetting his finger on his tongue and shuffling the money.

"Right. Exact amount," he beamed foolishly.

He almost rose from his seat with the two bundles of money in his hands, but then seemed to change his mind. He placed both bundles of notes side by side, took up the one on his left and began counting again. This time he counted in a sing song manner, like a child learning how to count. He went through the second bundle of notes as well in the same manner. He ended his counting and was about to take up the task again when Karen intervened.

"Could we have the receipt for the money? Now?"

The look of disappointment on Mr. Singh's face was apparent. It was as if a child had been deprived of his favorite sweets.

"Yes, yes," he replied absently. "You wait here."

He strolled over to the cashier, all eyes in the room following him as he took the few steps in that direction. The peon that had positioned himself at the next table jumped up and followed him as if it was his bounden duty to follow Mr. Singh everywhere he went.

"You from Africa?" the fat woman demanded from the far corner looking at Karen, the air having returned to her. "Where you get so much money from in Africa?" she shrilled.

A few grunts of satisfaction followed this comment.

"Africa is very poor country, no?" she was now warming to her subject.

There was no comment from either of the girls. Unable to attract their attention or provoke them into retorting she lapsed into Hindi. A few started to laugh at her comments. The man sitting at the table next to her suddenly said something in rapid fire Hindi that only a person fluent in the language could understand. The burst of vocal firepower was accompanied by sly glances at the two girls. Howls of laughter followed his comment. The girls didn't understand any of the words being thrown around. But the tone, the sidelong glances and the openly hostile looks in their direction indicated that they were the topic of conversation, and not a complementary one at that either.

It was always like this wherever they went. You didn't even have to look different. After all Iris, looked almost like an Indian. But if you were foreign and were classed as a foreigner, then you were considered foul and would have a whole lot of comments heaped onto you. You were also expected to know the language the moment you arrived.

"You can't speak Hindi?"

Alka looked surprised, when Iris had said she didn't speak Hindi and could she please translate what was written on the form she had to fill for her bus pass.

"You should learn Hindi before anything else. It's very easy. You can pick it up in a month," Alka said.

"You can't learn in a month and it's not that easy," Iris said smiling. "I started studying Hindi before I came here. Followed classes for almost two months but I can hardly speak," she added.

"Impossible! It's one of the easiest languages to learn," Alka said.

"So how many languages do you speak?"

"Hindi and a little bit of English," Alka replied a little embarrassed at this probing.

"But for you it shouldn't be difficult," she added trying to cover up. 'Why don't you start learning now? Go for classes," she said.

"But I didn't come here to learn Hindi and I don't have the time to spend learning Hindi while being involved in my course work. Besides I don't have money to pay someone extra to teach me something that I really don't need."

Alka walked off annoyed. That was the last conversation they ever had. The next time they saw each other along the corridor in the hostel Alka pretended not to recognize her even though Iris smiled. She merely walked on feigning interest in the air in front of her.

It would of course be slightly different if you were 'white'. Then someone would try to exploit you financially. Subtly get you to pay for their tea in the canteen, invite you to a party and ask you to bring the most expensive items on the menu, but all the time treating you with a sense of reverence. Was it the color?

If you were African or Asian it was different. The resentment flew high and was at its greatest. How could someone from the Third World have dollars to pay fees let alone any money at all? Of course no one would even dream of admitting that India was also part of that great big Third World and that there were pockets in India that were poorer and more undeveloped than those in Africa or any other part of Asia. But no. India was a great country. That was the usual parrot cry anyone would hear anywhere, for anything, anytime. Being a foreigner if you dared to even prove otherwise, let alone question the fact, you'd be lucky if they still acknowledged your presence let alone speak to you. And if, as a non white you pointed out a flaw in this great virtuous land brimming with corruption and violence, then you were doomed. Not a single classmate would help you find a book in the library or even tell you who had borrowed the book you needed.

Karen remembered the first day she entered the classroom someone had asked, "So how do you like India?" this when she had arrived only a week ago. She had told him as much and added laughingly, "Ask me that question in a month's time and I would probably be able to give you an answer."

The student that had asked the question looked disgusted as he huffed off without a second glance and never spoke to her again. In fact he did his best to ignore her even going as far as to avoid sitting next to her in class. She had become an untouchable overnight. And all because she was a foreigner. Was that fair?

"They really shouldn't admit foreign students if they can't accept them as humans," she told Annette one day.

"May be they should educate the average Indian about the world. Tell them that there are other countries besides India. Other people besides Indians," Annette replied.

"The next time someone asks you if you like India, just say yes. It doesn't matter if all you've seen of India is the inside of the airport. They just need reassurance that they are nice people and their country is the greatest on earth." Mike said when she recounted the incident in the classroom.

"Even if it's a lie?" Karen asked in surprise.

"Yes. Specially if it is a lie." Mike said firmly. "I do it all the time."

"But don't you feel like a hypocrite?" Karen asked.

"Sure I do. But I'm only here for a year and I don't mind being a hypocrite for a year."

He didn't sound in the least bothered about what others thought of him.

"You are horrible!" Annette exclaimed.

"I really have no choice. Try disagreeing with any Indian and see what happens?" Mike challenged her.

It wasn't only in class. Things were the same in the hostel. In fact it was much worse. The moment Iris entered the room she shared with an Indian student a whole bunch of other students sauntered in on the pretext of talking to her roommate. They planted themselves firmly on whatever available space and started blabbering, all the while staring pointedly at her. There would be laughter exchanged, not the kind of fun laughter, but laughter loaded with malice. Someone pulled out a piece of paper or thumbed through one of her books on the table without the slightest indication that she had no business to go through someone else's personal belongings without that persons permission.

After they exhausted their topics of conversation they stared at her. Just stared. No smile, nothing: like brain dead animals or a bunch of zombies watching TV.

Iris felt extremely uncomfortable the first time it happened a few days after arriving. But she soon grew so thick skinned that she glared right back at them the next time it happened. A real hard glare. That made some of them lower their eyes in embarrassment at being caught at their silly game and they left the room. But it was an ordeal. She consoled herself with the thought that she was in a zoo and looking at a group of curious baboons. This mental picture of primates in salwar kameez helped her laugh about it. Every waking and sleeping hour she had to be on her guard against students that were jobless with nothing to do but come in to the room just to stare at her even in the dark or fiddle through her possessions. It was weird.

One night Iris woke to the sound of a rat on the table. On opening her eyes she saw a covered form stooping over her table in the dark. She jumped out of bed and switched on the light scaring the intruder so much that she knocked a couple of books off the side of the table. They landed with a big thud on the floor. That woke up her neighbor. She rushed in to see what was going on. It also brought a few others from the other rooms. The intruder, a girl from one of the rooms at the far end stood staring, a guilty look on her face.

"What were you doing meddling with my things?"

Iris demanded crossly, but the girl didn't have an answer and slowly slipped out of the room before Iris could ask anything else. The other students stared at Iris as if she had no business questioning the intruder, made some rude comment in Hindi and left. Iris had resigned herself to accepting all this, but it was hard and she was slowly getting fed up of it.

"Just one more year," she kept telling herself. "One more year and you'll be out of here."

Meanwhile, she had to go through another one of those now familiar ordeals again in the Administrative Building of the campus.

ॐ

Mr. Singh returned with the receipts. The peon had abandoned him to stand at the cashier's door like a sentry guarding the entrance.

"This is yours. This one's yours," Mr. Singh said handing over the receipts to the two of them as though he were handing over the class prize.

"Thanks," they mumbled pocketing the receipts.

"You are enjoying India?" he asked, back to his conversational mode.

"No."

His face fell.

"But why?" he demanded in mock concern. "Is anyone trrarb-ling you?"

"Yes, people like you," Karen retorted and they walked out leaving a crestfallen Mr. Singh to answer all the questions from his colleagues.

The queue outside the room had not ended though it had trickled to a few people, may be fifteen or twenty students. It was twenty past twelve. When they arrived the queue was snaking itself round the room outside like a sleepy python and they had to push past the confluence of students to get into the room occupied by Mr. Singh and his staff. That was in the morning. Such a long time ago. Almost like another lifetime. Another day wasted.

"Let's get something to eat," Karen suggested. "We will have to wait till tomorrow to finish the rest. We'll never get anything done this afternoon."

The afternoons were also typical. Anyone would be lucky to find people in their prescribed place after lunch. Everyone vanished after the lunch break appearing for a few minutes at their table only to vanish again till tea time. The staff used their tea break as an excuse to sit talking over their cooling tea, and then it would be time to go home.

Ahmed bumped into them as they were leaving the building.

"You managed to pay your fees? How was it?" he asked.

But he needed no reply as the look on their faces told him all.

"I was there yesterday and they gave me a lot of trouble,' he said. "Why can't they get some sort of system to work out how and where we pay our fees without making us run around all over the campus and waste our time like this?" he demanded.

"These people will never learn," Iris said.

"This is India. Get used to it, I suppose," Ahmed added gloomily.

They sauntered across the large open space towards the canteen inside the building next to the classrooms. The sun was shining through the trees dappling the footpath with bright spots of sunshine. A bird was calling out in the distance; students were talking and joking all around. The afternoon breeze swirled trying to lift their dampened spirits. The girls felt relaxed. It felt good to be out in the open after that heated and unpleasantly heavy body odor filled room devoid of any ventilation. They breathed in the warm dusty July air and smiled for the first time that day.

They were glad to get their mind away from the morning's disagreeable encounter. Anything was better than the putrid air in that room.

On Death Row

᳚

The waters glistened slivery blue in the evening light. In the distance, the orange sun dipping behind the trees painted the sky in shades of red, pink, orange and gold before it began letting go of the day. The soft light caressed the breeze that lay silky fingers across the waters, trying to pick up small waves to dance with. The gentle wind rustled against the white clothes of the devotees who came to pay their respects, lifted the hairs of the people passing, and quietly followed the evening light as it stuck a long finger in through the open window to touch the hard uneven stone floor in the room where Gayathri Devi sat. She had been sitting here in the same place for a while, not caring about what happened around her. She'd seen the colors change in the sky a thousand and one times and more and was no longer interested. Was no longer overjoyed. She no longer anticipated the fading beauty of the end of the day as she did the first time she arrived.

The clouds drifted slowly up in the sky. Powder puffs moving unhurriedly from one side to the other, blocking the sun one moment only to show it the next as they moved lazily from here to there. The Ganga flowed gently below. If Gayathri Devi cared to look down from the window in the room she was in she would have seen an exact picture of the reflection of the sky in the river. But Gayathri Devi had no care for things like that. Not anymore. Not for some time.

Gayathri Devi no longer had any need for the beauty of nature. It all looked the same to her now. The beauty and the dirt all appeared identical. Her mind had ceased to notice the difference. There was no reason to look at anything or anyone. She had stopped looking and merely saw whatever was in front of her, never registering anything, not a shape, not a color. If things were there in front of her, she let them be. She didn't have the power to change anything. People came and went, the clouds drifted and the wind whistled through the open windows in the small room that was her home, but she found it hard to call it home even after all this time. She still clung to that tiny particle of memory that had the image of her home as she remembered it, a place with a small garden with marigold growing at the sides, an old worn mattress and pillow for her head at the corner of a room and food on a clean plate. This place she was at wasn't home. It was the only place she had to stay without being thrown out and for that she supposed she should have been grateful, but it wasn't home, merely a waiting room of sorts. Yet she had no choice so she sat there and waited. And waited. And waited.

Gayathri Devi was waiting to die. She had been here for a long time, but it appeared as though death was in no hurry to come and take her away. She had been hanging around for such a lengthy period she had forgotten how long. Sitting inside the small room on the banks of the Ganga she stared out into the open space. But although her eyes were looking ahead she barely saw what was in front of her.

Dressed in dirty white with her head shorn, she was one of the many widows shunned from her family and forced to live a non-existent life. She was like them all; no more than a shadow of the person they had once been. But a shadow that breathed and walked. Ate and drank. Slept and awoke to the call of the river, always to the call of the river flowing languidly below them, like it had been flowing since the beginning of time and would flow until the end of time long after everyone had left and the cities had crumbled and turned to jungle again. The women all waited patiently, lonely beings in the heart of the bustling city where no one cared about them. They were acknowledged as the women who had ended their lives and had nothing more to offer. It was time for them to die. So they were brought to the city of God to wait for His call. But He did not call and yet they lingered hoping He would appear and call them to Him. It had been a while since any of the shadows had made it to God's side. They had been waiting for so long they had forgotten how long. They no longer cared either as there was nothing left to be concerned about, only loneliness amidst the swirl of people that had no time for them, and sadness at their inability to live the life they had thought they would lead.

No one had prepared the women for this and although the women knew it happened, they had all thought it wouldn't happen to any of them. How could it? Those were merely stories they heard about people in faraway places, not about people they knew of. That was, until they became the characters in the stories they had heard about. Now they sat there trying to come to terms with what fate had stored up for them. Some of them, the older ones like Gayathri Devi had given up attempting to understand the reasons for being there, or for having to remain for so long until their time came to leave for good. But others, like the ones who had arrived more recently cried out at the unfairness of it all, imploring the holy men visiting the river to intervene with God on their behalf to help them leave. Yet there was only so much the holy men could do.

People fed them out of pity whenever they could. Pilgrims coming to visit the Gods city and bathe in the Ganga offered food to them in the hope of gaining some merit for their lives lived in the living. They also gave out of a sense of fear. What if their lives turned out the same? What if they had to sit alone like this and wait for God to call their name? Life was so uncertain and only God knew what it all meant. The pilgrims and people of the city gave whenever they could. But that wasn't sufficient for the lonely women that had nothing. Women that once had enough, but had lost everything and everyone they had in a matter of minutes. Women that were forced to give up out of a sense of duty to those that needed to continue. They were a burden on the young, an unnecessary life that needed to be cared for, fed, clothed and helped along the way. There was no time, no money or room left in houses for the likes of these women that passed their expiration date and were still sitting on the shelf, when whatever little money the families had were needed for the hungry mouths to feed, the demands of school and the dowries to be collected throughout their lives.

Women like Gayathri Devi were put aside and left to themselves and what better way to get rid of the unwanted than to send them to God. It was a little early no doubt, but they could always wait. Sit in the waiting room and pass the time until their name was called up. What did it matter when it would happen? It would surely take place someday. God would reach out to them when He felt it was suitable for Him. Until then they could wait. Sitting patiently in Gods little waiting room, waiting for the final call they could use the time to prepare for the great day. They could also use that time to pray for the well being of the families left behind in the village and request God to ensure that things worked out fine for them, make sure the harvest was bountiful, the rains came on time and there was enough money to feed the new mouths that were hungry. Always hungry.

No one in that vast city teaming with humanity coming and going daily bothered with the shaven headed women dressed in all in various shades of white. They were left alone to wander the narrow streets as they wished as long as they did not trouble or make unnecessary demands.

There were five women living there. They came from different places in the country, villages with strange names; they were brought there by a relative that left them in that small room. The relatives never visited again. There was no use. It was an expense. Besides, they were in God's hands now and who had the right to interfere in Gods scheme of things? If God wanted to keep them safe He would do so. It was His wish. The relatives left the women consoling themselves they'd done the right thing. The women sat in a small room open to all to see, above the burning ghat, waiting for their turn at the ghat. But their turn never came. Not in that moment, not the next but many monsoons later when they had lost any sense of reason for being, existing from moment to moment, waiting for the moment. Always waiting but never really certain.

The fires flickered on the bank at the side of the river as it always did. The shadows moved in silence in and out of the narrow alleyways, winding this way and that, but always leading towards the flowing waters below. The night closed in yet the activity at the ghats never ceased. The fires rose high lighting the night and everything around in a ghostly pallor. The crackle of the wood would sometimes break the stillness of the night although it bothered no one, not even the men tending the fires. Sometimes a splash of something falling into the water could be heard over the other noises or of someone treading the water at the river's edge, perhaps a late night stroller washing his weary feet in the rivers warm caress. Gayathri Devi could not see them, she could only hear. The light snaking out from the windows in the shops and houses along the bank was too dim for that and the light from the burning at the sides was not strong enough to penetrate to where the sounds came from.

Gayathri Devi sat at the edge of the room and gazed out into the murky waters, rippling here and there, lit up now and then by the glow from the fires. Ghostly lights. Flickering, rising, falling then disappearing into the sky leaving behind clouds of gray smoke that always had that strange smell. The smell of death that was stronger at night when the other smells of the day had ceased to be. No marigolds in baskets, no incense sticks perfuming the air, no odor of frying food, just the smell of bodies burning at the water's edge at night.

Not a single being could offer any help to her now. Gayathri Devi was all alone. She was like Revati the woman sitting at the open window looking out towards the other shore, seeing nothing in particular except the dark shadows of the shore on the opposite side. Gayathri Devi crouched in her corner and didn't bother to look out.

There was a time when she too sat at the open window staring out at the far distance, but that was a long time ago. She stared until her eyes hurt and the white light of the sun changed the shapes on the other shore into images of her life as she remembered. She stared and stared, from dawn to dusk, never missing a moment, as if taking her eyes away from a single instant would somehow stamp out the images flashing before her on the other shore. She watched her life as it passed in front of her like a film, showing her every second that she lived, the good, the bad, the happy and the sad. She relived them all sitting there staring at the invisible screen on the opposite side of the Ganga and cried in remembrance.

The last few days before she arrived were still etched in her memory and refused to leave. She found herself unwittingly taking herself back to her life in the village and the time just before her departure. That seemed to be the only fragment of memory that refused to leave her. She could still see the frail form of Krishan Lal as he lay on the old bed his body looking like a piece of old wood. When Krishen's condition worsened they couldn't do anything about it. He was old and bedridden and they couldn't afford to take him to the hospital. He died on his bed groaning in pain. It wasn't a happy departure. He cursed them all for his pain as if they were somehow to blame for his misfortune. He final words were a curse that pulled his lips to the sides in a grimace. The look of pure hatred on his face was not something anyone wanted to talk about or remember. Gayathri Devi had endured it all from the moment he became ill to the very end. The years of torment and the unspeakable agony of taking care of the invalid that was her husband had aged her. But she had to do it. There was no escape. It was her duty, they said. That was what she was born to do. Her children helped too, but they had their own children to take care of. The family barely had any money to cremate him. Gayathri Devi felt relief course through her veins when he died. It was as if a huge load was taken off her shoulders. She sat at the back of the house and played with her youngest grandchild. Life felt so much better. She felt as if a huge breeze lifted the sorrow out of her. She looked at the grandchild, her eldest son Ganesh's son and made plans for the time she would spend with him teaching him, singing to him.

But her happiness was tinged with sorrow. What would happen to him now that she was gone? She tried to picture him as she remembered, playing with the pebbles at the back of their compound. She felt pain at the sides of her eyes as the tears threatened to roll out. But there were no tears left to roll out. She had used them all up. It was as if her tear ducts had dried up with overuse and even forcing to create tears was an effort.

They had brought her here one day. Ganesh didn't want the extra burden. Money was scarce and they needed it for the child growing inside his wife womb. His wife would not be able to take care of the old woman and the other two children that were already there. It would be better for Gayathri Devi to be with God. There were rumblings that she too should have left with Krishen but she hadn't given much thought to these. They had whispered that she should have climbed onto the pyre and accompanied him, but she hadn't taken much notice of the whispers and no one had forced her. She remained in the house while her sons and the other men from the village took Krishan to the place they take all the dead. She had sighed in relief as they carried his body out of the small house. She was now free of the burden; free to live in contentment, she thought to herself as she huddled in the corner. Her sons would take care of her. That was what sons were meant for. She had given the family two sons. They would take care of her like they did their father. But here she was wrong. Very wrong. They both decided it was time she let go. It saddened and frightened her. But what was she to do?

Sanjay accompanied her to the Ganga a week after his father's funeral. The brothers decided he would take her to the Ganga on his way back home. The journey was long and Gayathri Devi was tired when she arrived at the river. She stood at the edge of the river and stared at the water wondering if she should ask Sanjay if he would get her a cup of tea before they visited the God's abode. Sanjay didn't want to stay to pray at Gods house, so eager was he to get away. He made some excuse; there was a bus that left in a few hours, he told her gruffly, refusing to look her in the eye. If he didn't take that bus he would have to wait for another week.

"Why beta?" she asked turning towards him as tears welled in her eyes.

Sanjay refused to look at her gazing beyond her towards the other side of the shore. She tried to speak, make him change his mind, but the words refused to come. She stared at him in shock as realization dawned on her. She opened and closed her mouth her lips trying desperately to form words that never came. She merely stood on the steps to the river and looked in front of her. She didn't want to see the guilt in her son's eyes. She thought they would be with her when she needed them most. When Ganesh had suggested she move to Sanjay's home for a while she had been joyful. Sanjay was the younger son and his wife had just given birth to yet another daughter. Although the birth wasn't what they wanted, Gayathri Devi was looking forward to seeing her granddaughters for the first time. She had happily agreed to accompany Sanjay to his home so soon after her husband's death. But she didn't realize what the brothers had in store for her until she arrived in Varanasi. She turned at the last moment to gaze at his departing form wondering if she would ever see him again. She didn't know what to do or where to go.

When her legs began to give way from standing she had eased her bag to the side and sat on a step leading to the river too shocked to do anything else. She remained there for a long time, until the movements around her ceased and the noise lowered to a whisper. Someone called to her and pointed at the room at the edge and told her to go there. Picking up the worn old cloth bag that held her meager possessions she made her way to the room.

Hovering at the open doorway she wondered what to do. Several bundles occupied the sides of the room, all dressed in old clothes that appeared as though they had once been white but looked soiled and stained. There was no place to sleep. The floor was dirty and she couldn't bring herself to lie down like the other bundles. She sat on an old piece of paper in the middle of the room hugging the old cloth bag and trying to sleep in that strange place with its odd mix of smells and noises, but the moment she shut her eyes she would feel panic rising inside making her throat dry and her head ache. That first night was the hardest and she was somewhat glad it ended, although the next day brought just as much gloom as the night.

She had come here with only a change of clothes. She didn't have any money or any food, except the few stale chapati she had brought with her from home that she hadn't been able to eat. She ate the old chapati, but after that she had to live off whatever was offered to her. Gayathri Devi was not accustomed to eating leftovers that were only good for throwing to stray dogs scavenging for morsels to feed their gnawing hunger. She had turned into a stray, a scavenger. She had become less than human and there was nothing much she could do to change that.

Soon Gayathri Devi took up the post near the window that looked out across the Ganga onto the other side of the river. The old woman sitting in the corner near the window had done her share of staring out at the world outside. She seemed to have tired of it and the waiting and never spoke to anyone. Gayathri Devi consoled herself. It was after all better to stay here than at home. This was closer to God. It would be easier to get to His place in the sky when the time came. He would see her better if she stayed close to His place on earth rather than inside her house in the tiny village that was hard to find. She brightened up at the thought and decided to ignore the low life she was forced to lead; the dirt, the squalor and the begging for leftover scraps of food. If this would take her to God faster then she would endure it all. So here she stayed. But the waiting seemed to go on and on.

She stopped counting the days after she counted the first year of Krishen's death. Time moved slowly, the days were endless and the nights more so. There didn't seem to be any respite. She wondered what her sons were doing. Had her daughter-in-law given birth to another son? What was his name? She longed for some familiarity, some comfort. Most of all she wished to return to her old home, but there was no way she could return. She didn't know how to get there. She didn't know where it was and had forgotten the name of the big town that was closest to the village. Even if she did remember she didn't have the money and most of all, she wouldn't be welcome.

There was nothing there for her. There was nothing here for her either. Only her frail old self and the white clothes covering her body that had grown brown with use and overuse. They hung around her like a limp rag. Her feet were as gnarled as the pieces of old burnt logs smoldering on the banks of the Ganga. The skin on her head turned coarse through frequent shaving. The stubble of black hair was slowly turning gray like her skin and her clothes. She stopped staring out at the other shore when the colors of the images turned to gray. Now she sat in the far corner like the old woman before her, away from the sun and the view of the river, waiting.

She had waited so long there was no telling what day it was or what year. She only knew His days as there were more people at the river, yet sometimes it was hard. There were always many people at the river at all times of the day. Coming and going. Some dressed in the most expensive silks, some in rags, some dressed in Sadhu saffron. Some walked, some hobbled with the help of a stick, or some youngster's arm, others were carried on a wooden frame wrapped in cloth and covered with flowers. Those ones never left. A part of them remained here forever. They would never go completely. One day she saw a piece of flesh cut loose and move downstream just below the surface. It almost knocked against the man standing at the water's edge, but he didn't notice it. There was always something floating on the river; marigolds, pieces of driftwood, pieces of flesh.

The smoke from the burning carried their souls up higher and higher. Or so they said. She didn't know what happened to them, she only knew what they said. And she believed this to be true. It would be what happened to her too. But the waiting was the hardest.

No one living in the houses that rose high above the river spoke to her or the other woman that sat inside that open house. They were the unwanted fragments of their families, like pieces of old furniture long past its use. They were left here to wait. No longer welcome, no longer wanted. They had come to accept this. But it was hard. Gayathri Devi's life had always been hard. From the time she was born right through to this moment. She had smiled on the day of her marriage but that too had been a half smile, a smile of trepidation of what was to come. There were no tears left inside her. She had cried them all just like all the other women had before her and those that would come after her.

Gayathri Devi had sobbed for every minute of her life that had passed. And when she could no longer shed tears her body cried out in pain, but she had tired of it all; she had become weary of the hurt climbing up her throat in a wail that would go on and on. She was all skin and bone. No more tears. Whatever was left was stored for the day when she would be free at last to leave. She huddled in her spot and waited. The film that had been playing in her mind's

75

eye had finally come to a screeching halt. It was the moment when she came here to wait. There was nothing more that she wanted to see or relive. Her life ended the moment she arrived.

I Exist. Therefore I Am

❦

I exist. Therefore I am.

But you don't know me. Not yet. Just because you can't fathom the depths or the panorama beyond the tiny margins you've drawn for yourself, or let others draw for you don't mean I'm not there. You can't see or hear me. I know where you are, but do you know where I am? I don't think you really know that either. That doesn't mean I don't exist, does it? It's just that you are unaware of me.

I exist. Therefore I am.

I rest deep inside you, wrapped up tight like an old woman swathed in quilts in the desert during winter when it's too cold to do anything but sit by the fire and wish it was summer once again. It's warm in here and comfortable and I'd like to stay. You don't know I'm here as yet. You can only try to guess, and maybe after some time you too will know I am here. But that would take time. For the moment, you don't know. Your ignorance is your bliss I will let you enjoy it until it is time to know.

I exist. Therefore I am.

How did I get here? That's a long story. I will recount it to you some day. Or maybe not. You may not believe me or think it is so. You've forgotten how you got there. You believe in something different now. It might cloud your accustomed thinking, confuse you as your ideas and beliefs do not provide for what I would tell you. You have become like one of them; all of them. You have forgotten. But I have not. At least for the moment I still remember. However I too might forget when I become like you after I've been taught to believe in the way things are and not what they really are. After all, I come to follow you. I know what you knew but have forgotten many monsoons ago. I know where I came from and how I got here. It's so simple, yet I'm sad since I know I too will forget all about it and spend my time trying to find out from someone that pretends to be knowledgeable, but doesn't know the direction his next step takes. That is my fate. I inherit what you give me.

I exist. Therefore I am.

In a few days you learn I am here, an alien being growing inside; a stranger. Someone you might get to know if you give us both the chance. But will you do that? More importantly, will they let you? You are happy. Everyone rejoices. I can't see or hear, but I can sense the reactions and feelings exchanged by all around you. Sitting perched on nothing in particular, I rejoice too. It's a good feeling to be content, happy, not have a care in the world.

I exist. Therefore I am.

I was but an idea that lived in the corridors of your mind a long, long time ago. I existed on a different plane, yet also inside the hidden folds of your mind that you kept wrapped up like a secret. How can this be, you may ask? That's how it is. It wasn't really I that lived inside your mind, but the germ of the idea that would become me when I left wherever it was I was at. The place I was in before I got here to you. The place I still remember but will soon forget once I get out of you. I waited there for a long time until it the moment arrived to depart and then I came straight here to you. Willed by what was to be. Your idea came to life. It was so simple. But it took a long time. That was our fault. We had to wait; I, because it still wasn't the right time and you, because you had to make the time for us. But it happened and here I am happy to be with you.

I exist. Therefore I am.

It was our combined karma that brought me here. Yours was the cause for my effect, but what it has in store for us is yet unknown. That is something that will play out as the days go by. It will be the result of our combined karma that will shape the story of our future. Right now I am really nothing much to look at. You can barely recognize what I will become, but I know, like the tree in the garden knows day must turn to night and night to day, that I will look a little like you. You see me through the folds of fat projected onto the screen and can only discern a small shape with a centre that beats like a drum. The sound and rhythm unlike the drums they played at your union, but a drum just the same. Thudak, thudak, thudak, it beats softly. You place your hand on your stomach but you can't feel me, nor can you hear the drum beats of my heart pounding inside me. Only the machine can tell you that.

I exist. Therefore I am.

But wait. There are more things you want to know. You don't need to know them, but all around they need to know, and you too have started on a quest to find out what you don't need to know but want to know urgently. For you see, I am just like you and will be too when I look into your eyes. This is something you dread. You don't want me to be like you; another image of yourself. You don't want to stare down at yourself in miniature waiting to grow, to blossom and dream. You would like it, I know, hidden in the tiny crevices of your mind you yearn for something like you. But all around they teach you that I should be like the other; different. That would be better. That's how it should be. You worry and curse and implore the Gods to give you the difference. Make me the difference. But the Gods don't hear you. Or if they do, they don't heed your call. A balance should be maintained, our karmic waves proceed the way it should. But you don't see it that way. You have grown up knowing something else, believing what they all told you. You have come to believe that what is right is wrong. That was how you were taught. You have been conditioned to attack your own image, to despise your own kind.

I exist. Therefore I am.

I grow inside you. I sense the meaning from your words, feel the fear threading through your veins and I'm tainted by it all. Is this going to be my lot in life? Your thoughts creep inside and strive to change the way I think. I make an effort to fight it off, but I'm not tough enough to stand against forces stronger than me. I can't push them away, and your thoughts and fears enter, turning me around, making me develop a little bit more like you every day. They make me feel uneasy even though I'm not sure why I should feel this way. I experience little waves of apprehension flow over me and wonder what it means for us.

I exist. Therefore I am.

They tell you they suspect I might be like you and your fear increases. It gnaws at the corners of your mind, the places that touch me and I too begin to dread what is to come. The food you send down to me is consumed with trepidation. It nourishes, but it too is tainted. I absorb the food of dread and foreboding and wonder what else will follow.

I exist. Therefore I am.

They take you in front of the machine again, but he refuses to tell you who I am although he can do so by just the touch of a button. He fears for me but is helpless to do anything because he is not the one in charge. The others surrounding you are in control and they are stronger. You go somewhere else; somewhere secret, where they will tell you who I am for some money. The family pays for this secret and you too agree. You want nothing of me either so you let them find out who I am going to be. There's silence all around when the machine predicts the truth that you don't want to know. Fake smiles hide the torment within as you leave the secret place. Fake smiles remain until you are home and the smiles turn to snarls. The ugliness is let loose. I listen to this, back and forth you all go trying to decide what to do with me. I will be a burden, I hear someone say. I will eat up all the money; take too much space in your life. Too much of your time and effort will be wasted on me while you can spend that time on someone else; someone different that could be better for all of you. I hear it, but you don't hear me cry or call out to you.

"Let me live. I want to live. I have a right."

My voice is too small. It is nonexistent to you. Or maybe you don't want to know about my decision. You place your hand on your stomach where I am as if to block the sounds of your words and those of the others, my family to be, from entering me.

I exist. Therefore I am.

It's my birthright to live, to be born, but no one sees it as such. I have become unwanted; a curse on a family that desires something different. Something everyone else has and everyone else wants. I am no one to them. They don't know where I came from or how I got here. They don't know what I will become or what I can become. They just know I can't be. It will create too much stress on a situation that shouldn't be; an expense on a family that doesn't want to spend on me; a heavy burden on a society that does not appreciate me. You pray to the Mother Goddess, to help you to be strong, but you have already begun to hate me. I can feel it seeping into me and I try to resist. I too cry out to the Mother Goddess to let me live. Who will She favor in this game of life? My voice is feeble and She may not hear my entreaty.

I exist. Therefore I am.

I have a right to be, but you want to take that away from me. I can't stop you. I kick out in protest, but it's all in vain. You don't know why I kick although you can feel it on your side. You don't know that I know what you are planning. Why am I cursed? Are you cursed too? You once went through the same thing. Did you hear them say the same things to you too? Back then you were lucky, the machines couldn't tell them about you; that you were different, that it would be best you shouldn't be. I'm not so fortunate. The machines are better now. The urgency to know your decision grows stronger and I await my fate.

I exist. Therefore I am.

They take you to another place where an old woman looks you over. She tells you what to do. You pay and leave. At home you try it all. Every single one of the remedies she taught you. I taste the strange taste you drink to put me to sleep. It turns inside making me sick but I'm still here. You can't chase me away so easily. I refuse to leave without a fight. It was tough getting here and I have no desire to go away. I'm strong although I'm still nothing. You continue to seek people who advise you to do strange things. You hurt with it all. You hurt me too, but that's your game isn't it? So why care if the tiny pieces of flesh that will become my arms stop feeling the way they used to. It's your doing, and the deeds of those who tell you what to do.

I exist. Therefore I am.

How can you hate someone inside you? Have they taught you something you have hidden inside a part of your mind that I can't reach, or is this really you? It makes me sad yet I don't blame you. It's what they tried to do to you too, many years ago when you were inside another. You fought hard to live and they couldn't prevent you from turning into what you are. But it was at a price. You lost something along the way. You don't know about it as it was a small price to pay for survival, yet the void is there for all to see. Maybe they know it maybe they don't. But it's there all the same. It could have got better, but they didn't care so much. They didn't want to spend extra on someone unwanted. They let you be. You had less to eat, the scraps off your brother's plate. He always came first although he arrived many monsoons after you made your appearance. You were never a number to reckon with; just a shadow that had to be fed. Your clothes were worn to the last thread. You were tired often, yet your spirit forced you on. And now see where you are; waiting to create. You should be proud of yourself. Instead they have made you feel you are of no use; a worthless person bringing forth a useless being.

I exist. Therefore I am.

Your hate grows. It's probably better this way. They did it to you since the time you were like me. Now it's your turn to bestow onto me my heritage; your hate. I tremble inside my little cocoon whimpering and wait my fate. Can I resist like you did and fight to the very last? Or will I succumb? Or be forced to give in?

I exist. Therefore I am.

You lie down on the cold hard table, a lonely figure in a long line of beings with no faces. They come towards you dressed in white from head to foot, their faces covered in purdah, their hands brandishing little weapons of destruction. Your fear spills into me as you see them. I experience the torment in you as you fight within yourself trying to decide even at this moment to resist, but they are too strong for you. They hold you down, give you something to numb the pain and you stop thinking. The weapons are thrust inside you. They touch, squeeze and maim. I scream in agony, but you can't hear me above your own screams. They pull out my arms; dig into my head. They keep digging into me, ploughing through me until I stop feeling. I'm no longer there. I watch you from above as they continue to pull me out. Little pieces of me cocooned inside you, still warm, still there. They scrape out every vestige of me that was inside you. I shed a tear. It falls onto your face but you don't feel it touch your skin as your face is already bathed in tears that flow into your hair and fall on the cold hard table. Slowly you sit up and someone helps you get off the table. You put on your shoes, pick up your things. The deed is done. They can berate you no more. Someone reaches out to you and you let them take you home. I have no home anymore. I was thrown out like a piece of stale old roti torn and disfigured, only fit for stray dogs. I stare at you leaving, your head bent, your hand on your stomach touching the place I was at not so long ago. I too turn to go. But we exit in different directions. You back to your home to find someone different and I go to who knows where. You think I'm dead but you don't want to mourn your loss. They don't tell you to either. There will be no mourning for me today, no lamps lit, no incense sticks burning into the night, no slokas chanted by saffron clad men. They are happy I'm no longer there. But I'm here, still very much here.

I exist. Therefore I am.

You read about the thousands like you that lose their way. There is nothing you can do. There are fewer numbers of ones like us being born. There is not enough to go around and very soon, much sooner than we think, there will be no one left for those to select from. That's what the papers say. But they still don't want us. How will they reconcile this lack of balance? Where will they find the numbers to compete? That is not something they want to consider. Better leave it to others to make. We will not bother. Too much time, effort and an unnecessarily expense that is best left out. You place your hand on your stomach and wonder. Is someone else waiting inside where I once was? Will this be the same or is it the difference they all yearn for?

I exist. Therefore I am.

Her Big Day was Fast Approaching

Shruti was getting married. At least that was what she continued to tell everyone she met. She had already set a tentative date. December 5th, the next year. It was almost February and this meant that she had exactly twenty three months to prepare for the marriage ceremony. This required a lot of work – she had to get rid of the dark patches under her eyes and three rolls of abundant fat, one from around her neck and two large salami sized rolls from around her waist and hips. She needed lots of money to pay for the umpteen numbers of facials, membership to the gym, health care and the "reduce ten inches in two months" program. She also wanted to buy new clothes. At least twenty suits, ten lehengas and several sarees, all to be worn for the pre marriage visits to friends and relatives. And then there was the dowry to consider. This had to be generous, she kept telling her parents, Her in-laws wouldn't think much of her if it wasn't. Besides, how could she find a good husband without a big enough dowry? And Shruti definitely wanted a good husband.

"Remember what happened to Ritu didi?" she reminded her parents, "Her dowry wasn't very generous and her in-laws are always complaining to anyone they meet about the small dowry she brought."

The dowry was a fact of life Shruti and her sisters had grown up with. Surrounded by families with growing daughters who lived in the same housing building, they often heard the dowry arguments, from the girl's side when she returned home to collect more, or from the boy's side when they demanded from the girl to bring more long after the ceremonies had ended and everyone had returned to their lives.

Ritu lived in the upstairs flat of their building. She married four years ago and went to live with her new family in Lucknow. Every year just before Diwali, she visited her parents with a request from her in-laws for gifts. They were not small gifts, but expensive ones. Ritu's father could never afford these requests; once it was a new car for her brother-in-law getting married in a few months, a new cooking range for their home and of course the request for numerous types of clothing for the entire extended family for the occasion. Another time it was money for the uncle's by-pass surgery at one of the expensive hospitals. The requests never ceased.

When she gave birth in the second year of their marriage Ritu was sent back home for the confinement with requests for more gifts, this time for one of her in-laws relatives. And in spite of all these requests, she still had to endure the daily humiliation of coming to her in-laws house with a small dowry. But what could she do? It was the way of the world and she had no choice but to lower her head and pretend it didn't matter. The two burner cooker, instead of the entire cooking range, one third of the money for the uncle's operation and a gold necklace instead of the car was insufficient for her extended family. They took it, but grumbled at the humiliation they suffered at the hands of Ritu's family.

Ritu cried a lot when she came home, but there was no comfort for her even from her own family. Her parents were annoyed to see her whenever she visited. They knew there was only one reason for her in-laws to send her home to visit them and this was for goods. It was a never ending saga. After the third visit, Ritu's father scolded her for coming home to ask for things, saying she should learn to manage with what she had. But it wasn't Ritu's fault. She would have been happy to live with the little they had, but it wasn't her place to make that decision. She didn't live in her own house where she could make the decisions. She lived in a joint family and as the outsider she was the brunt of all the unfulfilled desires of the family she married into. Although she was the elder daughter-in-law, she had to do most of the cooking and cleaning and other menial work the mother-in-law asked her to do. The second daughter-in-law was saved from this. She had brought in a very large dowry that impressed them all.

The only way to break the trend of subservience was to go to the in-laws house with a big dowry; enough to satisfy the in-laws needs. Shruti had no desire of doing hard work and expected her parents to provide enough to satisfy the in-laws into treating her well.

Shruti was a Punjabi Hindu. Her parents moved from Delhi to Chandigarh several years ago after her father bought a flat in the new housing complex in Sector 35. The Khanna's house in Delhi wasn't good enough to promote the kind of status they wanted everyone to know. The small two roomed flat in Karol Bagh, wasn't exactly what you would call luxury. It was comfortable after a fashion, but like any other middle class home the space wasn't sufficient for their needs. Besides, being in a housing building it was noisy. Everyone knew everyone else's business. There was nothing secret. All the walls and the ceilings and floors had ears.

The eldest of the three girls, Shruti shared the smaller of the two bedrooms with Anjali and Nandini, her two sisters. It was rather cramped with just enough room for one double bed and a small cupboard that was always overcrowded with clothes, and a table for studying. It was alright when they were children, but as they grew up the girls found it difficult to share the double bed, so one of the girls took turns to sleep on a mattress on the floor.

Her two brothers, Ajay and Sunny didn't have a room to themselves. They shared their parents' large cupboard to keep their clothes and would spread their bedding in the living room floor while their paternal grandmother, due to her age and status in the family, had the full run of the crumbling old sofa which still had traces of the polythene dust sheets clinging to it.

When Shruti was in the eight standard her parents decided it was time to return to their roots. Mr. Khanna had saved a little money from the occasional consultancy work he managed to get, and he decided to invest this in a house. Besides, he was getting quite tired of his wife's grumbling all the time. Poonam was from a family similar to his – they were from the same caste and village, but the difference was that Poonam's parents were better off than Jitendra Khanna's parents. Jitendra hadn't been too keen with the alliance as he felt a little inferior to her money and class, but his parents assured him it was a good match and, besides, he was a man and after they were married he could do as he pleased. However, while Poonam never spoke of the better life she could have led had she married someone better, the thought was there like an unsung Bajan hanging over their heads whatever they did.

She ran the house well, and gave him two sons in the first two years of their marriage. He thought he could continue with the good luck of the first two years, but for the next three years all they could produce were daughters, one after the other. After the third disappointment, Jitendra admitted defeat. He never said anything to his wife, even though his mother yelled at him for being a coward and not being stricter with his wife.

Poonam went about her work silently, cooking, cleaning, washing and taking care of five growing children that needed constant care. She accompanied them to school, did the shopping and looked after her mother-in-law who was never satisfied with anything. What her husband didn't say, her mother-in-law did. While her husband bit his tongue and did not utter a word of remorse to his wife, mainly out of fear that she would speak the unspeakable, her mother-in-law had no such qualms. Her tongue was as loose as her fading chiffon chunnis that kept falling off her shoulders more than a hundred and one times a day. She would not give up any opportunity to berate Poonam for giving birth to girls.

"A woman should have more control over herself. She should be able to give her husband what he wants. And if she can't, then she should pray to God that He gives her sons," she once told Poonam when Poonam asked her what to do about little Anjali's raging fever.

Poonam ignored her and instead sought her neighbor's advice on the health of her child.

"Your womb is unclean. It can only produce worms. You have insulted seven generations of Khanna's by producing these girls. You should have known what you were doing. And now my poor son has to kill himself to find dowries for three hopeless cases. Do not bring any of your mistakes near me. I have no time for them," she spat out at another instance when Poonam asked her to keep an eye on the two younger girls while she went to the shop across the road for some dhania.

She did not say anything to Jitendra when he returned home but served him his dinner as usual. Noticing no dhania in the aloo gobhi he mildly commented on the difference in taste.

"I couldn't go to the shop to get some as there was no one to take care of Anjali and Nandini while I was away," she said as she served him a chapati.

Jitendra looked at his mother questioningly but she pretended she didn't hear what they were discussing. Realizing it would be futile to get involved in the women's argument, whatever it was this time, he remained silent. However the incident seemed to have brought about a change in the relationship of the two women. Poonam never asked her mother-in-law anything. She didn't tell her anything either. Ponam took care of her mother-in-laws needs as she had been taught to do by her parents, but her outlook towards her mother-in-law changed. There was an unspoken fury in her eyes as she went about her work with a cold determination. She would ignore her mother-in-laws complains and shouts. It was as if the old woman didn't live in that house. And when she was forced to, she would give the old woman such a look of hatred that her mother-in-law backed down. Realizing that none of her tactics worked anymore, her mother-in-law grew wary of Poonam and decided to keep quiet. An angry peace was maintained in the house.

Jitendra began to notice the change. But he said nothing, asked nothing. When Poonam said she needed help with the housework, he agreed to hire a maid, although it would mean a huge pinch on his pocket. He started taking night classes to improve his English. He also started taking the money that was offered to him under the table, or between the folds of a newspaper by people like him that wanted a change in their lives. He made note of the files to be misplaced and on his way to the small pantry in the office, he would drop off the contents of the files in the dustbin, not bothering to even glance at the painstaking scribbles across the pages. This way he was able to pay for the children's school requirements as well as begin to put aside a little money for the girl's dowries.

The next thing Poonam asked for was to move to a better house in a better neighborhood. But he didn't have enough money for that as yet. He tried to reason with her but she only sneered at him.

"What about all that money my father gave you?" she demanded, at last giving birth to the unspoken. "Surely there must be enough to buy a modest house with that."

Jitendra said nothing. He walked out of the room with a defeated look on his face. Almost half of the money given to him by his father-in-law was spent on his sister's marriage ceremony. There was hardly anything left from the balance, as he had spent much of it on hospital bills and medicine when his mother had her operation. The little he had left was still in the bank, but this was not enough to buy a house.

He had on several occasions considered selling the block of land he had in Jallandhar, but wasn't happy with the offers made by his brother who had inherited the adjoining property. He had opted to remain in the village and look after the land while Jitendra and his younger brother took on white collar jobs in the city.

Like his wife Jitendra also saw the need for a bigger space to live in. His mother grumbled that she didn't like to sleep on the sofa and his daughters didn't let her sleep in their room as she made a lot of noise and they couldn't study at night and anyway there just wasn't enough space for another person in that room.

"Why do they need to study? All that studying will not get them a husband. In my day good girls stayed at home and learnt how to cook and clean, not waste time with books."

No one bothered to tell her that things had changed a lot since then.

Jitendra put more effort to his work at the office. By the time Ajay was in the tenth standard he had acquired a considerable amount of money through his promotions and other means. He was fortunate that he met Mr. Dhillon at an office get together. Mr. Dhillon got him some consultancies which brought in added money.

But the rates in Delhi were too high. He couldn't afford a flat let alone a small house in any of the nice residential areas.

"We can only buy a two bed room flat in Khel Gaon with the money we have, and I don't think you would want to move to that area," he told Poonam one evening. "What shall we do?"

"I want to live in a nice house in a nice area without so much noise and pollution. Someplace like my home," Poonam said, a faraway look in her eyes as she remembered the house she lived in until the day she was married.

"Why don't we move to Chandigarh? Houses aren't so expensive and you could also visit your parents more often," he said.

Poonam didn't object.

The next year they moved to Chandigarh, and though his job wasn't as good as the one in Delhi, there was peace at home. It was not possible to get a single unit house, but the flat in the housing complex was spacious and the neighbors were respectable and much nicer than their neighbors in the housing building in Delhi who were from various social backgrounds. At last the boys could have a room of their own and the girls didn't have to take turns sleeping on the ground. Ajay was now working at a private office in Delhi and Sunny was in his final year engineering. It was also time to settle off the girls.

Shruti and her sisters were brought up with just one objective – get married as soon as possible. Like any good Punjabi girl they took excellent care of themselves – dressed in the latest fashions and visited the beauty salon twice a month. Being the eldest of the three girls and the first to be married, Shruti was also able to buy the type of dresses she wanted, without having to resort to hand-me-downs, like her sisters. However her parents were always critical of the amount she spent on each dress. She didn't shop at the regular shops in Sector 22 like everyone else did, but bought the most expensive designer suits that were thrice the price of a suit the others bought.

She was influenced by the new friends she made in college. Being in college meant she had more freedom than her sisters and she hung out with her new friends at every opportunity. Her friends' parents were richer than Shruti's and could afford to pay thousands of rupees for a suit for daily wear. Shruti couldn't bear to be seen dressed in the cheap-looking suits. She couldn't discuss fashion with her friends and the pros and cons of dress designers if she didn't wear them herself. They hung out at the shopping centers and spent a lot of time at the cafés near their home and strolling around at sector seventeen, window shopping and checking out the guys, clothes and CDs, in no particular order. Shruti also hoped to start classes in computer studies at a centre close to her home.

All the while she prayed for a husband. She fasted on Mondays, abstained from meat on Tuesdays, salt on Wednesdays, sugar on Thursdays and only had water on Fridays. On the weekend she binged on everything edible except beef. She also went with her dadima to the mandir to do various poojas to appease the Gods in the hope of getting a husband real quick. Her dadima agreed to accompany the girl solely because it would mean getting rid of at least one encumbrance in that house. The astrologer that Poonam consulted said Shruti would be married within the next three years, and filled with hope Shruti began planning for the big day.

"I want to get married after Diwali so that it would be like going through one big celebration to another, maybe early December when the weather is nice," Shruti confided in her friends as they sipped coke at McDonalds, their favorite haunt.

"That is so cool yaar."

"Have you decided what you will wear?" Deepti asked.

"I don't know, probably lehenga. What do you think?"

"I saw some really cool stuff by Arpita at her shop. I think she is a really good designer."

"Yes she designed my cousin sisters' entire collection. She looked gorgeous in those lehengas. I'm getting a suit made by her to wear for Pinky's birthday party next month. Why don't you try her out sometime?"

"Is your suit ready, maybe we could take a look and Shruti can decide?"

"Let's go tomorrow. I have a fitting for the suit in the afternoon. We could go after class."

Shruti liked what she saw and ordered four suits. Just like that. They each cost several thousand rupees and would be ready by the next week. She could wear them to class.

"They're quite cheap, yaar. I didn't know she did such nice embroidery," she marveled.

When they saw what their sister bought, Nandini and Anjali also wanted new suits.

"No, we can't buy all three of you suits at once. Besides, Shruti needs to find a husband first, so the two of you can wait," Poonam told the two younger ones.

"And you," she said turning to Shruti, "Why did you have to get such expensive suits? You aren't going for any parties, where will you wear such luxurious suits? You should think of the expenses involved. We also need to spend for the marriage."

Shruti sulked. It was always like this. Her parents always wanted her to buy the cheaper stuff. They didn't understand that she had to look good in front of her friends too. Deepti, Karishma and Manjit all dressed in expensive clothes. They went to the same classes and hung out together at the same places. So how could she not dress like them as well? Besides, wasn't it her parents' duty to provide for her?

The next day, Aunty Poorna, one of the family friends living close by hurried to their house to inform them that Mr. Sidhu's son was returning to India for a holiday. It would be a good chance to meet the boy who was said to be studying at MIT in the US. The week suddenly got filled up with appointments to the salon for a facial, hair styling, manicure and pedicure. Everyone was excited. There was a buzz of activity in the house with everyone helping to tidy the place before the visit of the Sidhus.

The last batch of candidates Shruti had viewed weren't all that good and the Khannas felt they weren't suitable for their family. Besides they lived in the village and Poonam didn't want to send Shruti so far away.

"She is not used to village life, how will she manage?" Poonam wanted to know.

Her mother-in-law was unhappy with the decision. She had liked one of the families and thought nothing of sending her granddaughter to live in the village and do the housework in a house where there was no electricity or proper running water. The family lived close to the Khanna's ancestral home in Jallandhar and the old woman was very keen on the alliance.

"But dadima, I don't want to live in the village," wailed Shruti, "I will have to do nothing but cook, cook and cook for that family the whole day. My hands will become so rough."

Her grandmother gave her a horrified look.

"A girl should be prepared to serve her husband wherever he lives," she grumbled, "In my day we would never argue with our grandparents decisions."

"It's not your day now dadima. Things have changed. I don't want to be stuck in the village like a poor relative. I would rather kill myself than marry into a village."

"How dare you argue with me? This is what comes of sending girls to school. Pah, you are no different from your mother," the old woman spat out and waddled to her room.

The matter was dropped immediately. The other candidates were also dismissed as unsuitable. They were wondering what to do when the news about the foreign returned student brought hope and some quick planning among the Khanna's.

Mr. Sidhu was known to Mr. Singh, Poorna's husband and she agreed to play matchmaker. On the following weekend the Sidhus visited, but despite all efforts to please, the Khannas were left wondering what to do after the Sidhus left. The dowry they wanted was too much for the Khannas and Jitendra thought it better to forget the whole thing. But Shruti was adamant that they not let go of this big fish, like the earlier time with the Branch Manager of Vishal garments.

"Why don't you give him the dowry he wants?" Shruti demanded when her father mentioned they should drop it.

"After all, it doesn't sound all that much, and anyway you have spent so much on bhaiyas education as well. They will also inherit the house and your property in the village. So why can't you give me a decent dowry so I can find a decent husband?"

Her father was unable to answer this. It was true that Jitendra spent over seven lakhs to send Ajay to study in the US and was hoping to spend as much for Sunny when the time came. The two boys would also inherit the house in Sector 46 as well as the farming land in Jallandhar. But that was only natural. They were sons and why wouldn't parents spend on the sons. That was the way things had always been and would always be.

Sons would always remain in the family. They would carry the family name, build on the family's profile and invest in the family's future. Daughters, on the other hand, belonged to another family; their husband's family. They were merely on loan to their biological family until the time came for them to join their husband's family. And until such time, they had to be taken care of – fed, clothed, educated and made presentable to their husband's family. All the money spent on a daughter was money wasted because it would be another family that benefited. It was far better to use that money to educate the sons. Keep it in the family, as it were. Added to all of this the daughter had to be given a dowry as well.

By the time the dowry issue was discussed between the Khannas and Sidhus via the Singhs, the Sidhus lost interest in the alliance and began looking elsewhere. The young Sidhu would have been a good catch and the younger girls would also have benefited by having such illustrious in-laws, but this would have meant giving the dowry collected for all three to just one. What would they have done with the other two?

It was getting close to the deadline Shruti had set for herself and there was still no man in sight. She was getting worried that her clothes would start to look old and out of fashion, and more importantly, she would not be able to fit into them because she had a tendency to put on weight very fast. Her diets never worked and the work outs at the gym didn't seem to be having any outcome either. Finally when she had given up on her dream the Kapoors came like a godsend. Both sets of parents agreed to the match. The dowry was discussed at some length and a date was fixed.

Shruti got down to preparing for the wedding. She was thrilled that she was finally getting married. More workouts, more visits to the beauty parlor, more new clothes. But by this time even her mother did not care how much it was all costing. She just wanted the wedding over with. Mr. Kapoor wanted to have a very grand ceremony for all three events. Punit Kapoor was the eldest son, and every effort had to be made to make this, the first marriage of the family look good.

"We want to have the marriage ceremony at Hotel Mount View," Mr. Kapoor informed Mr. Khanna, "My brother and barbi are coming from the US after ten years especially for this. It has to look good."

Mr. Khanna calculating the cost for all this went quite pale. The ceremonies alone would cost almost as much as the dowry. He told Poonam and she decided to ask her two brothers to help with the marriage ceremonies. After all, it was their duty to help their niece in this hour of need.

Meanwhile, Mr. Kapoor was approached and asked if it would be possible for the cost of the ceremonies to be shared.

"After all it's your son too, and what would your brother think if you didn't spend a little on your son's happiness," Mr. Khanna commented quietly.

Mr. Kapoor knew he was cornered but he also saw the truth in what Mr. Khanna was saying, so he grudgingly agreed to this. He would have much preferred to have the Khannas bear the cost, but he didn't want Mr. Khanna or any of his family going around saying that he, Rakesh Kapoor, had not given a paisa for his own son.

The ring ceremony was quite a success. They were lucky to get the grounds close by for the dinner. A shamiana enclosed the entire ground providing a large area for the guests to mingle freely. It was a nice cool evening, the start of the winter season and the time for all the shaadi's. Even the in-laws were impressed by the care taken to organize the events. There was a lot of food, a variety of dishes both Punjabi and South Indian. Shruti wore a pale mauve suit with heavy gold accessories. Her younger uncle gave her a diamond set which she showed off to her friends and younger cousins proudly.

"Real diamonds, yaar. Can't you see the sparkle?"

The henna ceremony was also to her liking. The heavily worked orange suit that her aunt Shilpa gave her was admired by all. Shruti's sisters were also presented with suits in pale pink and green. All the relatives admired Shruti's pale wheatish skin, achieved through the latest skin whitening at the beauty parlor.

For her marriage, Shruti chose a salmon pink lehenga, on a design similar to the outfit Kareena Kapoor wore in her latest film. Arpita designed it for her along with all the other suits and lehenga's. Each lehenga cost an exorbitant amount of money. The one she wore on her marriage day cost over ninety thousand rupees because of the intricate beadwork and embroidery on the dress and chunni. Her uncle's were very nice and spent for most of her clothes and jewelry. Of course she heard that they grumbled and fought with her mother about the cost, but they had agreed in the end.

Her mother and sister also got nice outfits designed by Arpita. Her mother wore a chiffon saree in lemon green with zari work while Anjali and Nandini wore a red suit and orange lehenga respectively. Ajay bought her a small but rather trendy necklace. It wasn't very dressy but it would look nice to wear for parties. Shruti was very happy as her objective of getting married was finally being achieved. She sat inside the hall and waited for her husband to arrive, riding on his white horse and take her away to her new life. She waited a long time, looking demurely at her hands, weighed down by all the jewelry and heavy chunni.

The dowry issue was brought up again by Mr. Kapoor and his family just outside the entrance to the hotel and Mr. Khanna and his male relatives tried hard to persuade Mr. Kapoor to lower his demands. Mrs. Kapoor wasn't satisfied with the amount of jewelry Shruti was bringing and asked her husband to intervene and get more.

"The diamond necklace is very small. Ask them for something bigger, yaar," she said.

She also told him it would be a good idea to ask for a new TV, preferably a high definition flat screen that was bigger than their neighbors. As for Punit, he wanted a new car. His old Maruti was looking outdated and out of fashion.

"Her maternal uncle from Delhi can give us a new Ford," he told his father.

Meanwhile Mr. Kapoor's brother also wanted a new car for his son.

"It's hard for him to travel by scooter to college. The traffic in Delhi... You know how it is. The scooter is very old and breaks down often. We really need to get him something new."

So there was Mr. Kapoor proffering his shopping list to the Khannas right outside the hotel. Mr. Khanna was aghast. The TV he could manage but not the two cars. His brother came to the rescue and offered to give a motor cycle in the latest model for Mr. Kapoor's nephew.

"I heard the Bajaj model is very popular. Even my son was thinking of buying one and shipping it to the US when he goes for studies."

This impressed Mr. Kapoor who agreed to it.

"As for Punit, I'm sure his company can give him a new car. After all isn't he up for a promotion soon?" another brother piped in.

Mr. Kapoor felt a little defeated. He had boasted to all that Punit was going to be promoted to Director soon and would earn twice the amount he was earning. This had been the basis for the demand in the amount of dowry at the first instance. He could not say he made this up. Not now. So he nodded his head but stood firm about the jewelry. Mr. Khanna reluctantly agreed to give another diamond necklace. The men in the family shook hands. They patted each other on their back and laughed like old friends. The Barat was allowed to proceed.

Punit made his way slowly towards the hotel on a white horse. The band played shrill music as the family walked behind and in front of the hired horse. As they reached the entrance of the hotel the Barat stopped and some of the family members began dancing while Punit waited patiently to proceed. Dressed in white with a red turban framing his fat face he looked like any other boy on his wedding day. Punit wasn't very good looking. Nor was he very smart, but that did not matter. He was from a good family and it was a good match.

They were married without any more interference from the boys' side. Mr. Khanna and the male relatives of the family sighed in relief as the ceremony ended and the couple took off. They then began discussing how best to find the money for the additional items.

Anjali was next in line to be married and Jitendra's cousin had already offered to bring a proposal in the next few days. The year seemed to be a good one to get the daughters settled, but not a good year for expenses.

The newlywed couple honeymooned in Goa for a week and then they returned to Punit's parents' home in Delhi. Shruti was glad to return to Delhi. She had grown up here and didn't like the quiet lifestyle in Chandigarh. The Kapoors lived in a nice flat in Vasant Kunj and although it was very small it was sufficient. Punit's room was not very big and it now looked crowded. Punit's cupboard and table jostled for space with the new double bed and cupboards that Shruti brought with her as part of the dowry. They could hardly move around. They didn't have much privacy either, as his two younger brothers were always coming into the room to look for something or the other. The house was always busy, filled with friends or guests of the Kapoors. Punit's uncle and aunt had still not returned to the US and Mr. Kapoor was hoping that they would be able to help with their second son Abishek's education. He was applying for study in the US and it would be so much easier if he could stay with his uncle.

Back at the Khannas residence the girls were rearranging their room before old dadima decided to move in. Jitendra was looking older, Poonam noticed as she brought him his evening tea. He had a tired look on his face, like the times in Delhi when he had returned home late at night after work. Things had settled down in the house again. Everything will be alright, Poonam sighed to herself as she brushed a wisp of hair from her face and sat down in front of the TV.

Arti

Arti was in the midst of cooking the afternoon meal. There were only three of them today for lunch. She had everything she needed around her; dhal, potatoes, spices, methi and coriander leaves and the atta for the chapati. The chopped potatoes were in a bowl at the side and she was heating some oil for deep frying them first. The oil was beginning to splutter. She picked up the bowl with the potatoes and was about to add them to the hot oil when her mother-in-law left her post at the doorway and walked purposefully towards her. Arti was surprised. Placing the bowl back on the table she moved to the side. She opened her mouth to ask if her mother-in-law wanted anything when she spied the bottle in the old woman's hand. The look of puzzlement on her face turned to shock as the old woman came close to her, lifted her arm and threw the contents of the bottle at her. She smelt the kerosene before it even reached her and fear rose in her. She screamed and tried to get away, but the old woman pushed her back against the edge of the hard table. Arti grabbed the duster on the table and tried to wipe away the kerosene as best she could yelling and pushing at her mother-in-law standing over her, wondering how she could move past her to her to the door. Her mother-in-law took a step back and turned away. Could she make her escape? Arti pondered scrubbing furiously at her face with the cloth. Then her mother-in-law turned back, an ugly gleam in her eyes. Arti saw her mother-in-laws hands move to the saucepan on the stove.

"No!" she screamed in terror trying to push past her mother-in-law in that small kitchen. "No!"

But her mother-in-law seemed to have other plans as she picked up the saucepan with the hot oil and threw that too at the girl.

Arti screamed as the hot oil grabbed at her flesh and stung her eyes making it hard to see anything around her. She flung her arms out and tried to steady herself as the force of the heat threw her back in pain. She tried to wipe the oil slithering down here face with her already oily hands to no effect. The shock of having the scalding oil hurled at her and the agony of the burn coursing along her body was too much to bear.

"Ahhh..." was all she could utter as she tried to get rid of the pain.

Her chunni slipped off her left shoulder and trailed on the ground like a fat sleepy snake that didn't want to get up. All her clothes were bathed in thick scorching oil. Her hair continued to drip oil onto her face and body. It stung the front of her neck. Again she attempted to wipe her face with her oily hands, but it wasn't of any use. The oil burnt right through her clothes. Nothing she did was of any use. Arti cried in pain as heat entered her body cutting through her clothes and skin. It burnt a trail in search of her core. There was nothing she could do. She tried to walk, to run away, but the gripping pain slowed her progress. She was almost bent over as the ache gripped her being.

Guttural sounds like she had never heard left her mouth as Arti attempted to wipe away the scalding oil. She shrank back howling like an injured animal. But the pain continued. The older woman watched her crying out as she picked up the box of matches lying next to the old cooker. She opened the box and took out a match. She stared at Arti with an ugly look on her face. Arti cowered at the back of the kitchen as her mother-in- law struck the match against the side of the match box.

"No, no, noooo" she yelled in terror stretching her hands out as if to prevent the other woman from striking the match.

"No, don't do it!" she shouted, but in vain.

The matchstick struck out a little flame the moment it left the side of the box. Arti stared in horror as her mother-in-law lifted the flaming matchstick and with one gesture threw it at her feet.

The flame rose immediately. She smelt and sensed it near her. The flames caught her trailing chunni and moved up her legs, burning through her shalwar and torching her legs. The blaze leapt up to take hold of the end of her long braid of hair that was waving this way and that as she moved about in pain. Her hair singed with a sputter, sounding like the sizzling of mustard seeds in hot oil. But this was no mustard. It was her hair, her lovely long black hair.

Her husband's mother stood near the door watching, waiting. Arti shouted out angrily to her but she stood still, unmoving, waiting, the box of matches still in her hand. Arti screamed out a curse but the woman who made it happen was unmoved. She seemed not to care that the curse was directed at her. She merely pursed her lips tighter and stood where she was in front of the door, the box of matches gripped tight in her hand.

Arti burned with the full fury of the fire. She cackled and spluttered as the flames rose higher and higher on her body. Arti smelt the acrid smell of burning hair, strong and pungent over the burning fabrics. She felt the inferno engulf her from head to toe as she continued to run this way and that, screaming in desperation inside that tiny kitchen that had turned into a combustion chamber.

"Help," she called out in fear as she sensed the fire take hold of the hair on her head, "help me!" she beseeched turning around wildly as she tried to escape from the raging flames that engulfed her.

Yet no one came to her rescue. The woman that willed it stood silently at the side of the open doorway, letting no one in even if they wanted to and blocking the exit for Arti, willing the fire to finish what it started; waiting for the fire to finish its work. Arti cried bitter tears that were swallowed up by the flames. The skin on her face was quite burnt, it was stretched taut, her hands were the color of the night and her feet were beginning to look the same. Her arms were crusted with the remnants of her kameez that stuck onto her skin like a second layer of dark singed skin that could not be removed. She, whose skin was the color of wheat with not a blemish, was now brown and beginning to blacken as the red orange flames hissed and spat their way into her.

She rushed here and there trying to stop herself from burning but it only got worse. Coughing she searched on the table for the duster and tried to beat at the flames on her face, but it was of no use. It was more like an encouragement for the flames to burn more furiously. She threw herself against the kitchen cupboard, leaning back against it in the hope of stopping the fire from spreading, but the flames saw her move and turned towards her side. There was no getting away from their tentacles.

The flames danced gleefully as they rose up on all sides of her body moving higher and higher, growing stronger and stronger. They grabbed at her, greedily eating into her flesh through the burnt out fabric of her clothes stuck to her skin. The flames were trying to reach deep into her as they roared through her. The flames then began to spread around her middle. Her stomach was aflame and still they moved deeper and deeper.

Arti brushed her hands, already charred with the heat, against her stomach trying as best she could to prevent the fire from moving inside. She could feel the faint movement inside her being. It didn't know what was happening. Arti cried out helplessly, hopelessly, again and again, but her cries were getting fainter as the flames got stronger. She fell against the wall at the back of the kitchen and lay like a crumpled heap gasping and moaning, no longer able to speak except in moans, no longer able to explain except in sounds. She kept seeing the look on the woman's face and the utter hatred in her eyes as she laughed softly when the flames touched Arti's clothes running up towards her face. She was shaking with laughter as Arti continued to burn.

꿔

It was many hours later that they found her in the same heap against the wall. She had not moved an inch. The fire was doused; there was water on the ground and all over the kitchen tables to prevent anything from catching fire. It looked as though the rains had flooded the kitchen. There was water everywhere. But the water had not come soon enough for Arti who lay there on the ground amidst a pool of dark water. The fire was extinguished, but not before it had done what it was supposed to do. What all fires are supposed to do.

Mrs. Aggarwal living in the house next door heard the screams and called the police. The police were strangely prompt, but there was nothing they could do either. Mrs. Aggarwal hurried inside with them wanting to know what had happened. She was horrified at what she saw before her. She couldn't recognize the girl she was accustomed to seeing every day in the garden picking flowers. That girl was all radiance and full of life. This thing on the ground was like a piece of badly burnt toast; not good for anything except the dustbin. Mrs. Aggarwal stood in the middle of the kitchen in shocked silence.

"Wh...what happened?" she asked hesitantly turning around and looking at the woman that was still standing silently at the door, but there was no response.

Arti's mother-in-law refused to look either Mrs. Aggarwal or the policemen in the eye. Mrs. Aggarwal gasped in horror and covered her mouth with her hand as realization of what might have taken place dawned on her. She turned the other way as tears flooded her eyes and threatened to pour down her cheeks.

Arti's mother-in-law continued to stand silently at the side of the door without uttering a word. It was as if it was all too much for her. Nakul, her son was informed about the accident. He arrived minutes after the police and stood staring at the burnt out heap against the wall. He seemed unconcerned, as if it was not a person, not someone he knew, not his wife. He was annoyed that they had bothered him. He was at an important meeting, he said, and he had to end it abruptly. The people had come from out of town especially for that meeting. Now they would have to postpone it for another date, he explained in an exasperated tone. The two policemen exchanged looks, but did not say anything. The burnt heap was carried into the car and driven to the hospital some distance away.

The hospital staff received the charred body in silence. They were accustomed to seeing women like that come in every day from all parts of the town and even the remote villages that were scattered around. It was not something new. But this body was still feeling. They could hear the whispered moans coming from within. One of the younger nurses gasped and took a step back when she realized the body was still living and breathing.

Slowly the burnt out thing tried to speak. They could see some movement in the place where the face was supposed to be. Her eyes were wide open; the skin on her face was burnt so much it was hard to say if she could see or not. The police stood around her, her husband at her side. The nurses and doctors were in attendance.

"Maaji did it," Arti spoke through a disfigured hole in the brown lump, "Maaji threw the saucepan with the hot oil on me, then she lit a match and threw it at me!"

Her gnarled burnt body shook with sobs as she attempted to say more. She struggled to raise herself up to a sitting position, but could not. The tears coursed down her charred face as she continued to sob.

"Are you sure of that?" the policeman with the notebook asked.

He looked hesitantly at his colleague before opening the notebook and starting to scribble on a page.

"That can't be. My mother would never do such a thing. She loves Arti like her own daughter."

Nakul moved forwards and placed his hand on the policeman's notebook.

"She did, she did. Then she stood by and did nothing as I burnt," Arti cried out hoarsely, her voice growing weaker, fainter then turning into a whimper.

ॐ

Arti, the woman named after the flame was consumed by the flames around her. She dressed in red, the color of fire, of her name, on the day she married Nakul. Everyone commented on the effect of the bright red clothes that sparkled and shone brighter and more forceful than the red dresses worn by the other brides they had seen. The color was brighter than the setting sun. It made her pale skin glow. Arti looked a picture of radiance.

"You look beautiful."

Her best friend Madhu beamed at her.

"Yes, you look more beautiful than the sun," Sonali giggled as she adjusted the beautifully embroidered shawl on Arti's head. "Like a red rose, or the flame of the forest."

"Yes, didi, you look lovely," her sister Maneesha said looking at her adoringly.

Arti did look like a flame the day she got married. She stood out brighter than the fire she and Nakul walked around to seal their fate together in front of God and their families.

It was only a few months ago that she was shining with radiance. She no longer looked like that. No one would have recognized the charred brown thing that was lying on the hospital bed. A small portion on the side of her face near her jaw was saved. For what? Arti huddled on the bed whimpering to the air. The pain was so intense that after a while it became part of her. Arti's body was no longer of any use to anyone, or to her either. But her mind still lived. She contemplated about the life that she dreamed of in her home so far away. She remembered the day she looked like a flame, another sort of flame and remembered the admiration in her husband's eyes. But on the day he visited Arti in the hospital there was no admiration. There was no recognition either. It was as if she had ceased to exist; to him, to everyone else.

Arti lay there and saw her life play out in front of her. She had no one to talk to. Not here in the hospital, not in her new home. Arti married into a family that lived many miles away from all that was familiar to her. The town was crowded, but what town wasn't. She moved in to her husband's family home soon after marriage. Their marriage ceremony was a grand affair, lasting many days. She was happy to get married. Her family had found her a good match. Or so it was thought. Both families were content with the arrangements. There was nothing amiss.

But her happiness was short lived. Just like her life. Her contentment ended the moment she entered her husband's home. Arti was asked to do all the housework like a common servant. Her mother-in-law stood over her barking out commands, her disgust and contempt at the way Arti worked plain for all to see. But no one in her new family said a word. No one came to her rescue. There was nothing that could please her mother-in-law.

Arti remembered the incident that day. She was stirring the pot on the fire. The flames gently licked the sides of the pan as it heated the curry for their afternoon meal. It was an old stove and it was hard to cook on this. The new stove Arti brought with her as part of her dowry was given to her husband's aunt who lived in the next town. The aunt was always grumbling that she didn't have a good cooker. The old aunt was getting on in years and wanted something better than the old cooker she had. Arti's in-laws decided to give her the new cooker. Arti could use the old one in the kitchen. After all it was still in working condition. It would have been nice to get a new cooker, but what was to be done. The old aunt's needs were greater. Arti's face fell when she saw the old cooker. She tried to protest, but Nakul didn't hear of it.

"You can ask your parents to send you another cooker."

Nakul's mother said gruffly when she overheard the conversation. She stared at Arti with anger in her eyes.

"I used this cooker all these years and had no problem with it," she added with contempt. "You have to learn to live the way we live without having all those strange ideas in your head."

"Yes Maaji."

Arti obeyed the older woman and bowed her head.

She didn't say a word about the state of the cooker from that day. Nor did she say anything about the load of work she was burdened with. Arti tried to get accustomed to the ways of her new family. She tried very hard. But nothing was good enough for her mother-in-law. There was never enough salt in the curry, the chapati were never warm enough and the rice was never boiled enough. There was not enough sugar in the gulab jamun and not enough cream in the lassi. It was as if Arti could never do anything right. Her days were never happy. They were never without problems. She began to dread getting up in the morning. Her mother-in-law would be waiting at the doorway like a sentinel the moment Arti went into the kitchen to prepare the morning meal. She stood there and barked her commands, finding fault with everything Arti did, even the way she opened the tap to wash her hands.

After the first few months of marriage her husband also changed. He too began to see things that were not there. He pulled her up for not mending the tear on her kameez although it was too small for anyone to notice.

"Why are you wearing torn clothes?" he demanded, "You are the new bride of this family, do you want to shame us all by dressing like a servant? Haven't your parents given you enough clothes?"

Arti tried to explain that it was a very small tear, at the edge of the hem, but that had angered him. He slapped her across the face and yelled at her.

"How dare you talk back at me?" he shouted and roughly pushed her away.

Arti fell against the cupboard and injured her arm. She cried out in pain. But there was nothing she could do about that. No one took her pain seriously. After a while she kept quiet and didn't say anything to anyone.

Sometime that night Arti passed away. Nakul was informed about it immediately. All arrangements were made for her body to be cremated as soon as possible the next morning. It wouldn't be a difficult cremation. She was already half cremated. Why wait any longer? The police reported it as a domestic accident. No use in getting involved any further. The page in the notebook where Arti's statement was written was torn and thrown into the dustbin. The three thousand rupees offered by Nakul was more than enough for something as small as that. Everything returned to normal.

Arti's parents were informed a week later. They were shocked and came immediately to visit, to see the body of her daughter and pay their last respects to her. But there was nothing to see. It was already ash.

"It was unfortunate," Nakul's father said staring in front of him, "an accident. You know these young people never listen when they are told. The cooker was an old one and my wife warned Arti to be careful. But she didn't listen."

"But we gave her a new cooker!" Arti's father exclaimed, looking from Nakul's father to his mother, unable to figure out what had happened. "I don't understand," he said.

Nakul's mother who was sitting in the corner and observing all this made a strange noise as if she was trying to suppress a cough or a laugh. She placed a hand over her mouth and turned her head the other way but her shoulders continued to shake. Nakul's father refused to look him in the eye. After a while of staring in front of him he said slowly.

"Nakul's aunt wanted a new cooker and the girl was kind enough to agree to give her new one to the old woman."

He rose from his seat and walked into the garden.

A Chill Flew Across the Mountains

※

Cold winds raged across the valley as the sun blinked once then twice, turning the dark granite mountains walling them a deep shade of purple. All around her the mountains hauled themselves higher and higher until their peaks, covered in thick coats of snow, merged into the whiteness of the clouds roaming above and lost themselves in the sky. It wasn't easy to discern where the summit of the mountains ended and the sky began. They merged into each other forming a cloud here, a piece of sky there, and a reflection of something somewhere else.

Padma lifted her face to let the rough winds caress her cheeks as they passed by on their way to wherever it was that winds usually go. She stared out of the small window at the towering majesty of the mountains in front of her. Situated directly on the other side of the soaring wall of rocks, a half days drive along the winding dusty road that hugged the immense sheet of granite on one side and dipped down to the ice cold river flowing furiously on the other, was her village and family and all she was familiar with. But that place was many mountains away.

She had completely changed her life a year ago and had come to accept the life here in this lonely wilderness of strangers and their strange ways. She desperately missed her family but mostly she missed her old life, the freedom she had to do as she pleased; to live as free as the birds that flew like the wind soaring over the mountains, touching the snow peaks and descending to the river for a gulp of chilled water; just like the nomads that roamed with their flocks across the barren plains of Tsomoriri in and out of the country, one minute in India the next in China, with no borders to hedge them in. She wished she was a nomad. She wished she was home with her family; her real family. But most of all she wished she could change time. She rested her head against the thick wooden window frame of the tiny hut and sighed softly to the mountains. The winds snatched her sigh and carried it with them on their journey to wherever they were going that day.

Padma gazed out longingly at the mountains standing tall and unmoving, unaffected through time as people came and went, as ideas changed and life went on. But the mountains remained the same, or so it appeared. The winds fluttered about and the waters of the Indus gurgled through the valley as it flowed from its source somewhere hidden in the mountains to the end of its journey where it merged with the mighty ocean.

She couldn't believe she was home again. Much as she enjoyed the thrill and fast pace of the metro it was good to leave behind the dirt, dust and smog filled air and breath in the cool fresh breeze cascading down the mountains. Padma was pleased to be back although it was for a short time. Her sisters too were home with her parents and they were all getting ready for the impending celebrations. The annual festival of the Thicksey Gompa was popular and people came from all over the valley and beyond to participate in the festivities and enjoy themselves in merriment for a few days before the return to work. Padma's friends from the other villages were arriving soon and it would be a good reunion as some of them had opted to study at different colleges in different metros while a few had decided to remain in their villages.

Ladakh was also rapidly changing. Many outsiders, mostly Kashmiri businessmen were moving to Ladakh in large numbers. They had first come to run the tourist guest houses in Leh and to set up shops to sell their produce – pashmina shawls, crewel work cushion covers and wall hangings, carpets and religious knick knacks pilfered, some people whispered, from far and distant Buddhist temples that were gradually being abandoned. The numbers had increased year by year and there were now more outsiders than native Ladakhi living in Ladakh. The government was doing nothing to stop this migration and even though activists calling for unitary status for Ladakh were appealing to the central government to grant the territory the status of Union Territory, the politicians and other interested parties were dragging their feet. Meanwhile the migrations continued and with it the transformation in the lifestyle that was beginning to have an adverse effect on the way of life of the Ladakhi.

The Kashmiri were Muslim and their lifestyle was far removed from the Ladakhi who were Buddhists. Although the Ladakhi had at first welcomed the Kashmiri Muslims into their midst as they did to all who came to the valley, the rumblings of discontent were beginning to show. The Ladakhi were unhappy with the lifestyle and the drastic changes wrought on their simple harmonious way of life with the coming of the Kashmiri. They lived in the villages on the borders of Ladakh, but the effect was being felt even in the capital. The Kashmiri businessmen had come alone. They wanted a new life, but they were also reluctant to give up their old ways and embrace a new life. They wanted the villagers to change and adopt their life. The natives were being forced to embrace the ways of the outsider and many were unhappy. But they said nothing, did nothing. They waited hoping time would make the outsiders see that they were pleased with the way things were, happy with their lives and satisfied with what little they earned working the land in that inhospitable terrain. Neither the harsh winters that took over the lands for more than half the year nor the scarcity of water for cultivation in summer could deter the spirit of the Ladakhi people who were content to carry on as they had since time immemorial.

But the outsiders from across the mountain range were making things difficult for them to continue. It was strange how different they were. Centuries ago they too had been Buddhist, but a wave of Islam spreading across the region had converted almost all in the Kashmir valley and there was not a single Buddhist there anymore. Even the Buddhist temples were destroyed. It was not easy to be a non-Muslim in a Muslim land. The scattering of Hindu families that still lived in Kashmir were finding it hard to survive. Their lands were taken over, some were converted due to various reasons and others had left the valley in despair and chosen to live in the metros. They had become just another displaced people seeking a home in a tumultuous age. Would the fate of the Ladakhi Buddhists mirror that of the Kashmiri Hindus?

Padma met Niaz on the second day of the Thicksey festival. He was in his final year of study in Srinagar and came to visit the valley on the other side. He came with a few of his friends. They traveled by jeep across the mountains to Ladakh and stayed in a guest house run by a friend's uncle.

Padma and Niaz met many times during the festival and the days that followed both in Thicksey and Leh when she visited with her friends. When Niaz asked her to come with him to Leh that day Padma did not think there was anything amiss. Most Ladakhi boys had asked her out before and they had behaved in the utmost dignity with her. The Ladakhis were not known for taking advantage of their women or of saying one thing when they meant another. They were sincere in their ways and thought all others were the same; hence they trusted others easily without as much as the batting of an eyelid.

It was only a matter of hours from Thicksey to the city and she had made this journey numerous times. She could be back by evening, she thought. Salim drove while Amir sat in front. Naiz and Padma took the back seat. Driving along the winding road with the rushing waters of the Indus on the left Padma spoke about the life so different in the metro where she was based for her studies. Niaz had not been to the metro or any other big city, but he had heard it was different and he was making plans to visit the metro after he graduated. The road wound past Shakti and they stopped for a while for Padma to visit the Gonpa. Niaz and the others sat in the tea shop on the side of the road while Padma climbed up the steep hill to pray at the Gonpa. The boys did not want to enter the Gonpa as they were Muslim and didn't want to enter a non-Muslim place of worship although there was no restriction by the Buddhists. Anyone could enter the temples and Gonpas; it didn't matter what they believed or practiced. They were all welcome. But the Muslim boys didn't want to enter even though Padma called them.

"You don't have to come inside the shrine room if you don't want to. But come up. Come, you can sit outside and take in the view."

But they didn't want to enter through the temple door and made some excuse. Padma proceeded alone. After lighting a candle and praying for a while inside the dimly lit shrine she moved to admire the view from the side of the Gonpa. Padma stood for a moment breathing in the cool air and taking in the view like she had done many times before. Buildings looked like toys and in the distance the road resembled a long dark shawl weaving its way between the mountains and the river. A smile on her face she descended the steep steps to the road and they continued on their journey.

The otherwise sleepy town of Leh was brimming with life. All types of people walked the narrow streets. Locals from the villagers curious to see the life in the city, Indians from other states wanting to escape even for a few days from the heat of the rest of the country and many foreigners that came to visit the Buddhist temples and wait for the Dalai Lama who was schedule to visit later that year. It was an interesting town with an equally interesting atmosphere and Padma and her friends came here often just to walk the streets and hang out talking to friends from other villages. It was a familiar place to her. She knew every street, every building and every curio chop. It was a perfect day, but what followed was not like anything she expected.

The return home was not the homecoming she was familiar with or ever imagined. Nor was it the perfect end to the perfect day. Padma had heard of young girls from the remote villages who were abducted by men from Kashmir preventing the girls from returning to their villages for several days. When they did allow the girls to return the girls refused to go back out of shame. Neither did they inform the police or press charges against the men, reluctantly agreeing instead to marry one of the men. The girls' disappearance from the villages was termed as elopement and everyone kept quiet about it. They would later return as "married" women forced to wed a man they did not like and compelled to convert to a religion they did not understand. The girls' traditional ways were transformed forever. They had to adapt to the new life. They also had to adopt the alien religion that said women had no place in the world except as an object to a man. Padma never believed she would become one of those women. She never thought she would be so foolishly tricked into something like this.

How could she, a girl from a good family, who had evaded the ills in the metro become like this?

Padma couldn't bear to see her family and friends anymore. She felt so ashamed, so defeated and wronged, but mostly she felt insignificant. What could she do? Was this her karma turning? How could it have turned so bad? There was another girl, Dechen, from the adjoining village who "came" here several years ago. She was now pregnant with her third child. Her heart yearned to return to her home yet she could not even attempt to speak about it. She knew her family would take her back, but the shame of it all was something she didn't want to think of. Besides who would take care of the children? They were already destined to live as Muslims. There was no compromise. Dechen had to convert before their marriage. She was not allowed to practice her old religion. They claimed to be tolerant towards all religions but there was no tolerance shown towards her.

Padma's name was changed to something she did not like. A Muslim name for a Buddhist girl. She cringed every time she was addressed by the new name. Padma was the lotus; what more beautiful name could you give to a girl? Yet she was no longer the lotus that held its head high above the murky waters. She was now down below in the murky depths of the lotus roots, no longer to be called the lotus and move freely as the winds blowing across the water. She was a prisoner in the house. The doors were left open to let in the sun, the windows flung out wide to welcome the breeze, but Padma was not free to leave.

She heard of some girls that dared to return to their villages. Their "husbands" and their friends had followed and killed them all including their remaining families. Padma did not want to be responsible for the death of her parents and sisters. Neither did she want to remain here in this house nor bring to this world a being that would not be free to live like the wind.

The wind on this side of the mountain was not free either. It was forced to carry messages across the mountains on amplified sound. Padma listened to the words she did not understand as the wind droned on. She willed the winds to take her back, but there was only so much the wind could do. She thought of the prayer flags she had hung in the Gonpa's across the village and wished their prayers would come to her now. She could no longer show her face even to her friends. A dark shroud was thrown over her the day she entered her husband's house. She was no longer a person but a shadow that moved about like a ghost of her former self. Her mind was no longer free to discern, to think or to rationalize to be what she had been. It too was closed, caged in by the black shroud and not allowed to feel the sun.

Back in her village the people were getting ready to receive the Dalai Lama at his official residence in Choglamsar. Lamas swathed in bright red robes moved about making the necessary preparations. They worked with the villagers to erect tents around the grounds for people to sit under while they listened to the words from His Holiness, but every year there were a few missing people from the crowd. And each year the missing would grow in numbers. The Dalai Lama spoke of compassion and respect for all living beings to live as they preferred. Yet across the banks of the Indus a few feet behind his residence the Muezzin laughed at his teachings as it claimed yet another life.

Secrets

It was done. She could relax now. Deepti felt as if a heavy bag had been unloaded off her shoulders. She almost felt as if she would soar into the air like a balloon that has broken free from its string. Something close to a smile hovered at the corners of her lips as she sat, elbows resting on the table, her hands cupping her chin, and mused on what she had just accomplished.

It had taken a lot of effort and strength of mind to do what she did. But Deepti had ultimately decided this was the best way. She had told no one except Malini, her old school friend. Secrecy was the best in such circumstances. But the suspense had almost chocked her and she had been scared someone in the house would wonder why she was behaving in such an odd manner. But no one appeared to have observed anything amiss in her.

Her husband didn't detect anything and even her hawk eyed mother-in-law who knew about everything that took place inside that house was unaware of her state. It had been a grueling time; months of tension that had knotted in her throat and stomach, sometimes making it hard for her to swallow her meals. But Deepti had forced herself to be normal, reminding herself of her friend's words each time she felt her confidence slipping.

"Act like nothing has happened," Malini had advised her.

Deepti tried hard. It was crucial to remain calm and unaffected. It would not do for her husband or anyone else in the house to become aware of anything unusual in her demeanor and inquire about it. She was sure she would break down and confess if anyone questioned her or even made the slightest suggestion about anything being amiss. So she kept quiet and didn't defy her mother-in-law or get into any arguments with the rest of the family living in the house. Yet it took its toll on her mind. She was exhausted. It felt as if she had been stuck in a whirlwind and been flung out with her bones all beaten up.

But now it was done. She could unwind. Her lips stretched out into a wide smile, a real smile, as Malini placed the tray of food on the table and sat down opposite her. Deepti had not felt like smiling for a long time so anxious was she to complete what she had started. There had been times when she thought she wouldn't be able to go ahead with it but sheer determination and the silent support of Malini had helped. Malini gave her friend a questioning, wondering look as she sat down, but didn't say anything as she took a pastry from the plate she had placed on the table and began to eat.

Deepti too took a pastry and bit into it. It felt good. The soft pastry almost melted in her mouth as she munched slowly savoring the taste and texture of the food as it moved inside her mouth. A wave of warmth settled in and she felt a calmness she had never experienced envelop her. She leaned back against the chair and sighed loudly. It felt just like old times, before the friends had married. Life was different then. There were rules but they were different; they could meet freely as they wished without much of a problem or have too many questions posed by their families, unlike the families they had married into where the rules were different.

The restaurant they were in was noisy, but it was their old haunt and the girls felt at ease. This was the place they had come every time they wanted to celebrate something or share their sorrows. Deepti glanced around. It hadn't changed much. The paint on the walls had faded into a dull hue that was not altogether unpleasant. The tables and chairs were the same and they looked aged. Someone had attempted to carve out their initials at the edge of the table, but seemed to have given up after two letters. Maybe the place was crowded and the carver didn't want to get caught or maybe the owner had caught him or her in the act. Whatever it was the vandalism hadn't been completed.

Deepti smiled ruefully as she was reminded of a conversation during a visit when Revati had enthusiastically proclaimed she would carve her name on all the tables before the year was out. She never got the opportunity to carve even a single initial on a table.

Deepti was jolted from her reverie by the appearance of a waiter who placed two cups of coffee on the table. She stared at the steam rising from the cups then reached out and took hold of one. She lifted the cup to her lips and took a sip of the coffee closing her eyes as she followed the warm brew down her throat to her stomach.

She let her mind wander to that morning. The image of the diamond necklace lying inside that little safety deposit box brought a smile to Deepti's face. Her safety deposit box, her very own, opened under her name. Of course she didn't use the name she was known by. She used her second name Smriti and her maiden name Sharma. No one would even connect that Smriti Sharma was Deepti Aggarwal, the wife of Rakesh Aggarwal, the businessman.

The large diamond necklace sat in the middle of the safety deposit box – its new home. It was one of the many diamond necklaces that her family gave her when she got married four months ago. It was an heirloom that had been in the family for several generations. Deepti had last seen it around her maternal grandmothers' neck when they had visited for a cousins wedding. It had been gifted to Deepti's mother when she had married, but since Kavita didn't like the style she had left it with her mother until it was needed. It was passed down to the eldest daughter in the family. That had been the tradition. If Deepti gave birth to a daughter it would belong to her. If she didn't have daughters the necklace would go to her sisters' eldest daughter.

It had sat in a corner amidst the other jewelry that belonged to her new family inside their safety deposit box all this time. But it was now finally in its rightful place with Deepti's other jewelry. Soon all the other pieces she owned would join the large diamond necklace that acted like a beacon of hope. The necklace was the largest piece of jewelry and took pride of place among the rest. It was heavy and jostled for space with the other items of jewelry Deepti had placed in the safety deposit box. Deepti opened her bag and took out the key to her safety deposit box. It held her life in there. She clutched it tight in her hand letting the contours of it cut into her flesh. Malini watched her friend lost in her thoughts, but she didn't say anything as she too knew the significance of what Deepti had just done.

Deepti was glad to have a safety deposit box of her own. Neither her husband nor his family knew about this. Her own parents didn't know about it either. It was best they didn't know about as it would make things very awkward for all of them. She had gone to the bank with her friend. Malini too had a safety deposit box there under her maiden name that she had opened before she got married. Her husband didn't know about it either, just as Deepti's husband and in-laws wouldn't know about her deposit box. It was their secret. Something they would take with them to their death.

It became necessary to open a safety deposit box for herself, separate from that of her in-laws. Although Deepti had not given it much thought before marriage once she entered her new home she became aware about the acute need to have some safe place of her own. She had been a little amused when Malini told her she opened a safety deposit box before she got married. She couldn't understand why Malini would do something like that. She had joked about it then.

"Oh, you have so much jewelry it can't fit into one box!" she had exclaimed.

Malini had smiled and tried to explain, but Deepti wasn't interested. She merely grinned at her friend and waved her responses away.

"No, no go ahead. What a lot of diamonds you must have!"

But she began to understand why Malini opened a safety deposit box after she too married. It made perfect sense. She regretted not heeding Malini's advice earlier. Deepti had wondered for a long time what she could do about it. No one inside that house would help her. She couldn't trust anyone. They were her new family yet she would always, always be the stranger. There were rules in that house, like every house and she had to obey them like her other sisters-in-law. Rules kept the family together, rules made things work the way it was supposed to. But for Deepti the rules were too much. They were unfair and some didn't make sense. She felt stifled.

The dinner at the Khurana's, the Aggarwal's family friends, gave Deepti the break she had been looking for. She wore the small diamond necklace gifted to her by her uncle for the dinner. When they returned home it was late and Deepti put away the necklace inside an old hand bag she used to keep her handkerchiefs. No one would bother to look inside that, not even her sisters-in-law. She decided to wait. She would see what happened. Her mother-in-law didn't bother to ask her to return the necklace to the bank the next day or even the day after. She was disinterested or maybe the old woman had forgotten all about it. Deepti waited. The next week there was another party to attend; Rakesh's business partners were hosting a dinner for someone from out of state. She informed her mother-in-law that she needed her emerald set to go with the green saree she was planning on wearing. She wondered if the visit to the bank so soon would trigger any memories from her mother-in-law, but she didn't appear to recall anything.

The old woman accompanied her to the bank that day too. She had the key to the family safety deposit box that held all the jewelry they owned. Each woman's jewelry was placed inside that deposit box. It didn't matter which one of them the jewelry belonged to. They were all there in that one box that belonged to the family. Deepti opened the box and rummaged through the contents for her necklace.

Everything was a mess inside as everyone had placed their jewelry there one on top of the other. There were so many pieces all belonging to someone or the other. No one seemed to own them individually; they belonged to the family and although they were given to the women by their respective families when they got married for their personal use, it wasn't always like that. Deepti had not worn anyone else's jewelry, but her two elder sisters-in-law didn't confine themselves to their own jewelry but wore anything that took their fancy. They even fought over who wore what. Deepti silently hoped she wouldn't come to the stage when she too had to fight to wear what was rightfully hers.

She had placed her jewelry at the back of the locker a few days after the wedding ceremony, but it had moved to the side. Deepti searched through the other pieces of jewelry and found the emeralds she was looking for. She took out the necklace and matching ear-rings and bracelet. As an afterthought she also took out two other heavy gold bracelets she wore at her marriage ceremony. She had her back to her mother-in-law and Deepti surreptitiously wrapped the extra items she took in her handkerchief and transferred them to her handbag, closed the box and smiled at her mother-in-law standing by the door. Her mother-in-law hadn't questioned her about the diamond necklace she took the previous week. She had evidently forgotten all about it. Maybe she would forget about this one too.

Deepti didn't bother to return the emeralds to the locker either. It nestled next to the diamonds inside the old handbag in her clothes cupboard.

A few days later another member of the family made the journey to the bank. Her elder sister-in-law needed jewelry to wear for an evening out with some friends. She went unaccompanied. Deepti paced the house nervously wondering what would happen when Jyothi, her sister-in-law noticed the missing jewelry. She played out the possible scenarios in her mind and tried to work out some excuses that would convince her in-laws. She was so worried that she could barely drink her mid-morning tea. She sat with the rest of the women of the house and nervously sipped her tea. The women were talking about the latest episode of the TV serial they had seen the previous night and were coming up with possible scenarios for the next episode, but Deepti barely listened, merely pretending to be interested and nodding her head occasionally at something that was said. Her heart began to pound loudly as she heard the door of the car bang shut and footsteps enter the house. She could feel the thud, thud of her heartbeat move to her head and was almost faint with anxiety Jyothi went to her room to leave her things. Then she joined the rest of the family in the kitchen for tea. She hadn't noticed the missing necklaces. Deepti sighed softly and stared at the tea in her cup. Things were getting too hard to manage. She had to do something.

Four months after getting married Deepti made an excuse to leave the house unaccompanied. It was hard getting her mother-in-law to agree to it. Deepti had not stepped out of her husband's house for anything without being accompanied by someone; her mother-in-law, elder sister-in-law or one of the younger sister-in-laws. It was as if she was a prisoner in her own home. She was allowed to go on her own if she was going to places that were close by or that would require her to be away for a few minutes, like the little shop at the top of the road. But if she wanted to go out for shopping or anything else she had to be accompanied by someone.

Deepti spoke about Malini and how much she would like to meet her again for lunch like they used to meet before she married. Her mother-in-law had listened to her talking about this for many days and when Deepti had finally asked her mother-in-law if she could go for the day the older woman had agreed although she had grumbled a little. It had not been difficult because Malini's family was known to Deepti's in-laws. They had done business at one time and Deepti's mother-in-law didn't think anything was amiss when Deepti asked to meet Malini. After all what could happen? Malini was also from a good family like theirs and would not do anything in any way to bring shame on the family name. The mother-in-law agreed to let Deepti go unchaperoned but little did the older woman know what was going to take place.

"I took the other diamond set out of their safety deposit box last week. After going to the party I didn't return it. I didn't bother to go to the bank either," Deepti said between munching on her pastry. "The woman didn't say anything."

"Are you sure she won't notice it?" Malini asked looking at her.

"I will wait and see what she says. If she asks me what happened to the necklace I will tell her it's still with me and I was waiting to return it after the dinner that's next week," Deepti said. "If she doesn't notice I will not put it back," she added.

"But won't she notice its missing when she goes to take something?" Malini asked.

"Last month I took another small necklace and didn't put it back in. She came with me to the bank to take out the necklace but didn't bother when I had to return it," Deepti said, "I told her I had to return it and she merely gave me the key and asked me to put it back. But I didn't. Why should I? It's my necklace that my parents gave me. Why should I keep it in her deposit box?" she demanded sounding cross.

"But where did you keep it?" Malini asked, "You shouldn't keep it in the house. She might see and wonder why you are keeping it in the house. And then you'll be in trouble especially since she told you to put it in the bank."

"Yes, but I don't think she would notice. The first time I took out the necklace I returned it. She came with me and she saw me placing it inside the box. The next time she didn't come with me but asked me to take it. Then after the party when I wanted to return it back she gave me the key and asked me to put it back. I did. But last month I decided not to return any of the jewelry but keep them all with me," she said.

Malini looked concerned.

"There's so much of jewelry there no one will notice what is what. Everyone's jewelry is in there. I don't want my diamonds getting lost. The large one is a family heirloom. My family heirloom, and besides, my parents gave the necklaces for me to wear and not for the others to wear. I don't wear their jewelry, so why should they wear mine?" she demanded.

"The old woman wears your necklaces?" Malini asked amazed.

"Not her, but the elder sister-in-law. She liked the design of one of the necklaces and wanted to wear it for a party. But I said I hadn't even worn it as yet and said some shit like it was not right for someone else to wear it before the owner had worn it. The old woman also agreed. I mean, can you believe it? I have just got married and can't wear my own jewelry?" Deepti said a note of annoyance in her voice. "It's like a prison there. Everyone has to do what the old woman says."

"Be careful. Be very careful. Don't take everything out at once. Leave some there. If you take all out they will suspect something and you will get into trouble," Malini cautioned her.

"No I won't take them all out. There are some smaller sets, but I'll take the big ones out. I will keep them with me. Not in the family's deposit box," she said swallowing the last of the pastry.

"Thank you for helping me to open that box," she added gratefully, "You don't know what this means to me."

"Oh, don't mention it. I really do know what it means to you. It's the same for me too," Malini added, "the safety deposit box has been a godsend to me."

"Yes I can imagine," Deepti said, "It feels like a load off my shoulders."

"You shouldn't take all out though. I know it's your jewelry, but what happens when you want to wear it? You can't be coming here all the time?"

Deepti thought for a while.

"Yes, you are right. I should keep the one's I don't wear often like the heavy sets only and let the rest remain in the family's box."

It was like a floodgate had been opened. Deepti had kept it all inside all this time and it was a relief to be able to share her thoughts freely. It felt so good.

The girls continue to eat in silence.

"But why can't I take them all?" Deepti asked in exasperation. "I've a good mind not to keep any of it there for that family to decide. I heard that my mother-in-law had sold a necklace that belonged to Bhaiya's wife," Deepti said. "She hadn't even asked my sister-in-law, but had merely taken out the necklace and sold it saying they needed money. Can you imagine that? And it was a diamond necklace too."

"But what would you do if the old woman wants to sell one of your necklaces and doesn't fine them there?" Malini asked with alarm.

"I won't say anything," Deepti said, "the old woman had better answer to that. After all she is supposed to come with me to the bank whenever I go to take or return the jewelry. If she doesn't accompany me, or doesn't bother to check if I really put them back when she does accompany me, then she can't blame me if the jewelry is missing. She can't blame me as there are so many that use that box. Any one of them can take jewelry and not return. Not just me. So she can't blame me," Deepti said then added as her friend looked at her with concern, "Don't think I haven't thought about this thoroughly. I know what I am doing. Don't worry. No one will find out."

Malini sighed. It was the same for her too and she empathized completely with her friend. At least her mother-in-law didn't interfere as much as Deepti's. Malini was allowed to keep her own jewelry. But she had to keep it inside a small box that was then placed inside the family's safety deposit box. She didn't have that much right to her own things, but it was definitely better than Deepti's. Malini kept some of her jewelry in the small box inside the family's safety deposit box while the bulk she kept hidden inside her own personal secret deposit box. She also kept money. There would be need for that someday.

"You should keep some money aside as well," she said as she sipped her coffee.

"You think so?" Deepti looked concerned.

"Well you never know, do you?" she said, "Can you get money for yourself?"

"Not much. Not really," Deepti said, "I can take out small amounts from the shopping, and I do have a few thousands, but it's not enough. The money my parents gave as dowry was deposited in an account in my name. But the in-laws know how much there is in it and if something goes missing they will wonder."

"Well that's ok. At least it's in your name and they can't withdraw it without your permission," Malini said.

"No they can't do that," Deepti said.

They continued to sit there even after their meal was over. Deepti didn't want to leave the place. She was feeling so relaxed and didn't want to return to her in-laws home just yet. They ordered another coffee and continued to sit there watching the people come in and leave after their meal.

"Life is so hard," Deepti said after a while.

"Yes it is."

"Do you ever get used to it?" she asked turning to her friend, but Malini only sighed. A look of sadness crossed her eyes, but it was so fleeting that Deepti almost didn't see it. She opened her mouth to ask what the matter was but decided to let it go. There were too many things that didn't make sense and far too many problems they couldn't solve. It was best to toss them over and pretend they never existed. They both lived in different worlds controlled by their in-laws families. The world they knew was a different one, one they could only step into for brief forays, for short visits to coffee shops, an occasional hurried lunch at a restaurant or a few minutes conversation over the phone when the doors of the strict world was creaked open for a little while and the rules could be pushed aside.

Deepti sighed and smiled at her friend. The clock was ticking. It was time to end their visit. There was danger in prolonging the visit as unnecessary questions about what they were doing for so long in a restaurant would lead to too many lies trying to cover up and that in turn would lead to suspicion. None of them needed that now. They both stood up as if knowing it was time to leave. Outside they parted with a hug going their separate ways to the lives chosen for them.

About the Author

Shirani Rajapakse is a Sri Lankan poet and author. She won the *Cha "Betrayal" Poetry Contest 2013* and was a finalist in the *Anna Davidson Rosenberg Poetry Awards 2013*.

Her collection of short stories, *Breaking News* (Vijitha Yapa 2011) was shortlisted for the *Gratiaen Award*. Her poetry collection *Chant of a Million Women* (self published 2017) won the *2018 Kindle Book Awards*. It also received an Honorable Mention in the *2018 Readers' Favorite Awards* and was chosen as an Official Selection in the *2018 New Apple Summer eBook Awards for Excellence in Independent Publishing*.

Rajapakse's work appears in many international publications including, *Flash:The International Short-Short Story Magazine, Litro, Silver Birch, International Times, City Journal, Writers for Calais Refugees, The Write-In, Asian Signature, Moving Worlds, Citiesplus, Deep Water Literary Journal, Mascara Literary Review, Kitaab, Lakeview Journal, Cyclamens & Swords, New Ceylon Writing, Channels, Linnet's Wings, Spark, Berfrois, Counterpunch, Earthen Lamp Journal, Asian Cha, Dove Tales, Buddhist Poetry Review, About Place Journal, Skylight 47, The Smoking Poet, New Verse News, The Occupy Poetry Project* and in anthologies, *Fireflies & Fairy Dust: A Fantasy Anthology (Eu-2 2018), Flash Fiction International (Norton 2015), Ballads (Dagda 2014), Short & Sweet (Perera Hussein 2014), Poems for Freedom (River Books 2013), Voices Israel Poetry Anthology 2012, Song of Sahel (Plum Tree 2012), Occupy Wall Street Poetry Anthology, World Healing*

World Peace (Inner City Press 2012 & 2014) and *Every Child Is Entitled to Innocence (Plum Tree 2012)*.

Rajapakse has a BA in English Literature (University of Kelaniya, Sri Lanka) and MA in International Relations (Jawaharlal Nehru University, India). She worked as a journalist, researcher and an international development specialist before becoming a creative writer. An animal lover and vegetarian she loves to travel. Rajapakse lives in the suburbs of Sri Lanka's capital Colombo.

Thanks for reading!

Please add a short review on Amazon, Goodreads, your personal blog or any other book related site and let me know what you thought about the book.

Read *Breaking News*, my first collection of short stories, is set against the backdrop of war torn Sri Lanka. It was shortlisted for the *Gratiaen Award* in 2010. Or, if you prefer poetry, check out the critically acclaimed *Chant of a Million Women* (self-published, 2017). The book won the *2018 Kindle Book Awards,* received an Honorable Mention in the *2018 Readers' Favorite Awards*, and was chosen as an Official Selection in the *2018 New Apple Summer eBook Awards for Excellence in Independent Publishing*.

shiranirajapakse.wordpress.com

amazon.com/Shirani-Rajapakse/e/B00IZQRAOA